To Karl,

with my best
wishes.

This isn't one of the stories
I remember

Robin Wyatt Dunn

JOHN OTT

SAN DIEGO, CALIFORNIA

2018

ISBN - 978-1-940830-24-7

LOC - 2018939249

Cover art by Barbara Sobczyńska

By Robin Wyatt Dunn

POETRY
Poems from the War
Science Fiction: a poem!
Sunsborne
Wine Country
What Black Delirious Daylight Sets You Forward in the Boat
Remarriages
Debudaderrah

NOVELS
Los Angeles, or American Pharaohs
My Name is Dee
Fighting Down into the Kingdom of Dreams
Line to Night Island
A Map of Kex's Face
Julia, Skydaughter
Conquistador of the Night Lands
White Man Book
Colonel Stierlitz
Black Dove
City, Psychonaut
2DEE

SHORT STORIES
Dark is a Color of the Day

PLAYS
Last Freedom

FILMS
A Wilderness in Your Heart
Party Games
American Messenger

for my mother

Feed me the liquid night that I've been longing for; dress it over my luminous eyes; over my hair, over my skin; around my balls; sketch me in the street of Los Angeles, a city whose name no longer means what we thought it meant--it's getting a new name--name me, tonight, when I am born, for you, again:

Send it fire and sweet calcium, to stage my shaking bones:

You could send it over

You could sketch it out, around my legs, over my hat, in the air around the buses and the people of this city, slow and so angry we can barely speak:

Feed me black lagoons and broken mirrors broken women in Hollywood feed me Chinatown dreams and Koreatown haircuts feed me black Sundays and hearsay, beating the door; beat my door for me; beat it down; I'm here.

Beat my lagoon with your delicate hands; raise my match over my face;

Hello!

It's good to see you here. I thought I might be the only one around here. But now I know there's you. You've been here. I thought . . . but never mind. We're back.

This black time ain't easy, in part because it looks easy. People look at this part of America they think it's easy; they think we don't feel any-

thing; don't notice anything. That we're all blind.

But we're not.

It's just we can't talk about it. Someone's got us by the throat.

I could kill you too; I know. The city does it to us, makes us its slave. Puts its thoughts in our heads.

But we're stronger than it is; bigger; more magnificent. More glorious than a city.

Bigger than the universe.

No universe is like Los Angeles, seedy and alone on fire, thrumming with fire, liquid limn patting the noose with fire, over your eyes and your hair, through your ass and your bare skin, in your heart. Bigger than the universe is our heart; bigger than Los Angeles.

Blood for you.

Take me with you; where you're going. I promise I'll be useful. I can kill. And I can make new friends.

Part 1

1

This isn't one of the stories I remember.

It started when I was five, and my people were back at home. They'd been to the city, and received bad news. I was on the synthesizer, practicing my trumpet.

I can see my father's face, grim and harried, and shouting, not at my mother, but just in the telling of the story, of what had happened. I don't remembering what it was. Likely he'd been put out of work by one of the new arrivals. Or it could have been something else he'd seen, in the city that was coming to be.

Of course, it's still there. I lived there many years, and am now considering going back.

But I don't want to remember all of the things that might entail. I'm sure you can understand that. It isn't even that memory is a burden. No, the problem is that they're no longer my memories. I don't want to remember them wrong; so I might as well not remember them at all.

I have a dix-huit sur vingt grade on my Lunar Composition #7. I am invited to play for the CEO. He is having a party at his villa, on Sondern Street, after the fireworks to celebrate our victories.

What we have been victorious over this year is not what they say, of course. We've been killing each other. In secret.

t's not talk about that. I need to speak to
other things. Revolutions come and go, but
 is something which I still believe has meaning exterior to politics. But it's also possible that
my discovery may help to save my family. Despite
everything, all of their betrayals, I suspect that is
what I've been moving towards this last year; a
kind of jailbreak.

To shutter them out of the dream into—

"Robert? Is it you?"

She's standing very close to me.

"Elizabeth, I didn't know you were home."

"I'm not, this is one my new holograms. Are
you writing something? Who to?"

"Oh, it's nothing. A poem or something. I'll delete it."

"Don't forget to let the dog out."

He is sitting at my feet. Not interested in going
out. For some reason Benjamin is immune to the
hologram's eyes. Dogs are special after all; they exist in worlds we cannot.

"I have an appointment at six," she's saying.
"Do I look okay?"

"You look beautiful," I say, which is not a lie.
Liz uses fewer of the artificial enhancements than
is customary these days; she has a rebel streak in
her, which is probably why I love her. Despite ...

Well, it doesn't matter really. Marriages can be
the pits, as you may know, and this particular one,

my second, is only incidental to my work now. She is more than I deserve, perhaps, but she is also simply far removed.

It's just dreams; that's the work. It sounds silly, I know. I don't even have the right equipment. But that is by design. We don't even know what the right tools would be to answer the questions I am interested in. The brain is tool enough, for now. Mine is still working! Ha ha.

"You should delete that poem, Robert. They get in the way."

"Yes, I will."

"See you soon."

I blow her image a kiss mid-air and watch as the static covers her up and she fades.

Benjamin is licking my leg, and I scratch his head.

"Shall we take a nap?"

He moans.

I lie down on my bed, in the dark room, and close my eyes.

ɔeen getting trickier. This part isn't
ɟined. Well, that's science. We call it
⸃ something else ... no different than
a dream, really. Dreaming, as I've come to understand it, is a kind of lens. One which you can focus.

My dream self is in an office, working on a
poem. Outside, in fantastically bright yellow sunlight, skimpy trees shake in the wind, and brightly
polished autos blind me through the window.

Things haven't been right for a while now; I've
gone back in time, in this series of dreams. I've ar-
ranged for me to wake up in three hours but I don't
know if that will be enough time ...

Two sets of voices are engaged in argument,
at an angle I cannot see below my window. One
speaks in English; he sounds African-American.
The other is shouting in a different language; perhaps Vietnamese—it is hard to hear over the traffic.

There is a node here I will be able to use, if I
can find it. I call them nodes now: places or events
that overlap between my dream life and my waking.
The nodes are important, but I don't know much
more than that. Hence my science experiment.

The node is in a building. Over the glow of the
summer city. I can feel it. Like a small gravity well.

Or an electric transmitter. I have to go to it but I'm stuck to my chair, in the dream, writing this poem.

Well, I might as well write it then. Perhaps the dream logic will let me stand up and start my search if I finish it.

Patient fellow
Lurid god
Wimp in the wind.
Take your bow and usher off the stage
All your events
And make room for your wake
Of reality

Not very good. Is it a good thing that language is inexact, or a bad one? And is scientific inquiry the same way?

Below, a bright red car is accelerating towards a bicyclist ... I lean out the window, to shout? The cyclist hears me, he turns his head, and collides with the hood of the car, and goes flying through the air ...

I am screaming but I can't make a sound.

3

Benjamin is licking my toes. The room is so hot I can barely breathe. I turn on the environmental conditioning and check the power levels and ease back into the bed. Benjamin regards me warily. His look says "I don't want any part of it."

He's a smart dog.

In the kitchen I can hear Elizabeth. I want to rise and greet her but I feel stuck in the bed.

Maybe I'm depressed. But that condition is no longer recognized in the psychological manuals.

In my dream, I was drinking water so cold it made my teeth hurt. I can still feel the delicious pain ...

I get up and walk out to greet my wife, drenched in sweat, the dog following slowly behind me. She gives me her killer smile. I feel certain she would kill a man wearing exactly that expression.

"I got the contract. We're in the money for nine months."

"That's wonderful darling. You earned it."

"Did I wake you up?"

"Thank you. I needed it."

"You've been sleeping too much."

"Probably."

4

I've been disingenuous, though perhaps that's the point of these things.

The sun has come up, and I've been waiting. On what I don't know.

There is a lyric energy to it; these discoveries. Uncovering things. It seems innocent, though it isn't. It isn't harmless. No information is idle, or uninterested in you. But what does it mean, Robert? Explain yourself.

I had thought I could still make this a story of the revolution; and I do want to. You can see our society has crumbed; made all kinds of horrendous mistakes. Turned us into almost-robots, and all sort of other things. The shadow of the real ...

Well, I'll tell that story too perhaps.

You see, I want it to make sense. And there's no other way to do that but to tell it my own way, though I wish it were different. I wish this story were neat as a bow, and that God had told me to write it, and everything were clear as day. Although that sounds horrible too. Still, it would be a good story. One I could remember properly.

This story is also from memory; but one that is only now coming to be. One of the consequences of my experiments is that I've taken an unusual position in relation to time. Not that it goes backwards, or that I'm outside of it, or even that it's jumbled. Just oblique. Time skids around a bit now, and it must have something to do with my dreams.

Well, I should have begun this way:

I can no longer tell the difference between sleep and waking.

I go to sleep in both places, and wake up. And just like for "normal" people, there isn't always a clear relation between the two. Though we say there is. We say that it all works out like clockwork. That we're these happy machines ...

I understand Proust a little better now; that urge to create the universe out of language. Otherwise, it must hardly exist.

There are other things at stake too. And knowing that is all that gives me the strength to continue this narrative: the belief that it does have some higher purpose. Not God, but other people.

You other people out there! Well, come along. I'm sorry it didn't happen sooner. I'm sorry it wasn't clearer. I wish it could have been. And I wish that I were stronger and that it would be all right in the end. But I'm not sure that it will be. Likely we'll be changed. But that's all right.

Hold my hand now, and step into the abyss ...

5

Water. It's like that now. Foul and damp. But you can appreciate it, in the blackness. Sometimes I come here to remember how it was, before the aliens came. Before I knew all the things that I know now.

Hahaha!

You can drink it; it's all right. It's just very cold. But pure. Over there is my cave. You can see the fire; they keep it lit for me. I'm some sort of sha-man to them, or perhaps a god. Actually I've no idea what I am to them. We don't know each other very well. They're modern day cave men. Like us, you see?

Just on a visit to a nuclear shelter under a moun-tain.

Here, sit against the rock with me.

It's been a long time. I should like to give you my data. It's why I'm writing this.

I am a scientist; I'm sorry if that wasn't clear before. It's still a new profession, you know? We're making it up as we go ...

My specialty is consciousness.

I've come to think of it as a road. Probably Proust would agree with me there. Maybe Beckett would too. He loved roads, Beckett.

I know one of the chief difficulties of my endeavor though. While I believe in my story, I don't believe enough in my scientific project.

Roads don't obey scientific laws as we understand them. So I've been trying to suggest the outlines for one or two new ones. Map these whereabouts, if you like.

It's all very much connected to what you want: many other branches of science understand this now too. What you are interested in finding indeed affects the experiment. It doesn't mean you'll find what you want, but it will change what you find.

What is the relation between the two? My hunch is that it is similar to the division between dream and waking.

But I'm taking too much; likely you're hungry. Let's go eat with the cavemen; likely you'll startle them less than I do.

Here, they're inviting us. I told you they're friendly. This is Monica; although I can't pronounce the name in her language. She always likes feeding me. You'll like it, I promise.

It's hot, isn't it?

I'm going to sleep soon. Hold my hand, won't you?

6

My father was always very kind to me as a child. Perhaps that is part of my problem, that I have been unable to summon enough violence to destroy the system which is degrading me. My upbringing continues to nourish the deep instinct towards kindness which our current world does not seem to know how to accommodate ...

The city was destroyed. My father's. Mine too. It is still there but only as a ruin. I wouldn't go there if you paid me.

I see what this story is now: a war survival story. I should have known that, but I'd forgotten.

Typically the logic of these stories is: nothing is the same. All is lost. But some redeeming characteristic, perhaps, may be divined as a jewel from the chaos.

I am fond of these stories; they are heartwarming and thrilling.

They remind you how fragile reality is.

Few of them, however, try to understand the war itself. It is usually taken as a given, as part of life. Its cruelties are to be endured, or avoided, or confronted. In many of them, war is presumed to be, ultimately, incomprehensible.

I am tempted to adopt that logic ... perhaps it would be good if I did.

But this story is not about punting the difficult questions.

Even if I am a mad scientist, I am still a scientist. I am doing it for you. So that you will know what I have found.

The experiment is narrative itself.

If the story succeeds, and if it can be repeated, new knowledge will be gained.

I am going to sleep.

Good night.

7

The problem with beginning a ⌐
of narrative is that we have no idea what time is.

Space is puzzling enough, but Newton and Einstein did manage to photograph that dimension for us, with their minds.

No genius photographer has arrived, to my knowledge, to do that for us for time.

A study of narrative can begin with the simple acknowledgement that we are ourselves the subject of the study. We are not designing this experiment but it is being designed on us.

Already this realization is helpful for understanding experiment itself: the outcome of any experiment, it follows, depends on the will of both the experimenter and the experimented. Even as nations' fates depend both on kings and slaves. And as with kingdoms, while it is tempting to regard them as top-down power relations, the feedback loop is anything but. They are fused together, the master and the slave. God and Man, experimenter and experimented.

Joined into the reality we are in the process of constructing.

Dreams and waking can be understood as the lenses on this project of experimentation. Two modes of interacting with the world. Two laser beams who heat the air, synchronously, firing in rhythm, in order to elicit some heretofore unseen reaction ...

Some scientists like to talk about their work as though it is separate from the rest of the world, some private temple closer to God than the rest of us.

But empirical means at root, experience. All experiment begins right here, wherever you are.

Your life is an experiment with matter.

8

Heal me, in this midnight, where I am come, though I had known nothing, and will never know anything, and though this night is poison, and you may be poison too, I will deliver to you what I have promised.

This terrible midnight poem, burning inside me.

There is no midnight, and no light, and no reason. There is the presence of divinity, useless, and lingering, gone.

I have arrived. Never again. I am not arriving. I am gone.

That's all right. My words are here, though I am dead.

A miracle.

Goodbye, and hello. This music is something I've put on, to help me through the agony of this story, though it perhaps should be easier, and I perhaps should have made allowances for it. But what allowances can one make for a story?

You can edit it, cut it down afterwards, but that is only after you have heard the story. There is no editing a story in hearing it.

You can make no allowances for a story. It is allowed everything. It is permitted everything. It is all powerful, in the universe where it exists.

Well, so we say. It may even be true.
Thank you. I believe I know where to go next.

9

I have begun, much too soon. Let us say I am a child; take my hand, through the warzone.

They are bombing.

Bum, bum bum, bum. One two three one two three one two three, here under the wall.

Wait it out. See the lights trembling down? The aliens do it. Firing from so far above ...

Have you ever seen a man die?

The silence afterwards is beautiful.

I can control the aliens, did you know that? I can drive them out of the sky?

"What do you mean?"

They listen to me. They're my friends.

"Where are we going?"

California.

10

My wife is gone. I pace around the house. We do not subscribe to any news services. When you leave the house you will learn whatever it is soon enough.

This is a gift. That I should be so insulated, and that the world should be so eager to inform me of everything as soon as I step outside.

I have not been outside in two years.

It is not that I am agoraphobic. Though we have no true agoras—open markets—anymore. It is simply a question of risk management. My work is risky enough.

In the 20th Century, the phrase "thought experiment" denoted a kind of risk-free zone, a Reading Rainbow time-out, where anything could be possible, and very little was risked.

Now we know that thought experiments are the most dangerous kinds of experiments.

One step too far, and you can be in for a set of very grave surprises.

The dog is a hologram but he has a personality. I watch his eyes.

"All right boy?"

He makes a low moan. I put his dish on the floor and the hologram pretends to eat.

Inside the refrigerator is my coffee. I like to

drink it cold in the summer.

Outside the window, the city is burning. It has been burning for thirteen months.

11

Perhaps I am outside of time after all. Or perhaps we are all outside of it. I need to decide my goal. How far I believe I can make it before they shut me down.

12

We are walking through the rubble.

The pigeons, eating grass, watch us with something like love, and pity.

Moving into the everlasting night.

Carrying my fiddle.

I have been carrying my fiddle a very long time. Someday, I believe, I will play that fiddle at court. And it will be glorious. Someday I will be transformed, from this boy, into a man, full of fire and fury, knowing all that I will need to know.

The burning grows in me, a fever, till I lance it, with this recording.

Tell me how it goes; how will it go. What will you do.

Who is hurt and who endures, who makes and who sticks the stick into the ground, to look for water, or just to say that we came through, under this dusty sky.

Refugee is not the right word. We're people. There is no refuge from this.

We're moving like our ancestors, through the black water and the burning sun. Looking for answers. Reasons. Doubts, and dribbles of clean water, stories from the fire and waste, and the look of children, thrilled to be encountering the world, in its hazy glory.

We're moving north. Like Moses. But our only god is one another. The mountains are distant; invisible behind the haze.

13

I am dreaming. My right foot balances over my left. The night heavy around me. Inside my head, that hollow music waits for the nightmares to start.

When I was a child I would dream of the beach. Bright blue. Now I dream of a sea again, of space, stars stretching over my head, through me. Underneath me.

Still I can see the city burning. And a woman is singing an elegy; her child is dead.

I go to the refrigerator and pour more water. The hologram dog watches my face. I rustle my hand through his digital-blue hair.

This entity in me—what I am, or who, the being and the present, beckoning me in—it sits at the bar and I drink the water, cold and flat and quiet. The entity in me is dreaming.

I feel the world, inside the edges, underneath my feet, and underneath my scalp, turning under my skin, turning the darkness behind my eyes, and spreading them over the room, which vanishes, in blackness.

Now the soundscape is empty.

"Still awake, Dr. Renault?"

"No, I mean, yes. Is that you Alice?"

She watches me from the door. "Do you want me to turn the lights on?"

"No, that's all right. I was just leaving."
I step outside, into London.

14

I am the subject of an experiment. But I am also performing an experiment. This is the nature of experiment. I live above Piccadilly Circus, in a small room.

It is not as nice as my dream apartment.

Still, this one is real.

When I was a child I survived the destruction of Ypres; its second great destruction. Now I call London my home. I have even stopped speaking French.

Inside Ypres, the darkness reminds me who I have become: its benefactor. Its messenger. Its thing, on a string.

15

I can hear the guns churning; and they will never stop firing, not as long as I am alive.

Over the French mud. Inside of my head.

What is the nature of dead weight? And why do so many enjoy imagining the worst?

I am in my favorite café. Wood and glass and steel and afternoon light. Soft voices and no music; only the distant sound of traffic.

My superiors tell me the experiment is going well, but this only because VR is still a heady phenomenon; they could care less about the actual experimental goals of the project; they just want more people to live in simulacra.

In a way I do know what they mean, though. One gets emotionally attached to one's imagination, even if it not quite "your own." And then the real world seems slightly more distant ...

"Is this seat taken?"

"Um, no. Please, sit."

She is perhaps thirty-five. Looking dangerous. "What's your name?" I ask her.

"Elizabeth."

"Do you live in London?"

"I live upstairs, actually."

"I've never seen you here."

"You're that scientist who was in the news."

"Yes, I may be."

"Living in your dream world."

"Yes."

"Can I visit your lab?"

16

I show her the room. None of the furniture is new. It looks like a beat-up community theater, with lots of green screen tape over everything.

"You're writing a story about our work?"

"Mmm," she says, looking through the lens of her camera.

"And what's your take?"

"Don't have a take, exactly. Just wanted to see it."

"I've worked here two years now. This particular narrative line is now six months old. We had tried a few other stories, but this one is producing better results."

"You're married, in your story?"

"Yes."

"But not in real life."

"No."

"That must be funny."

"It doesn't bother me. It's no different, really, than anyone else's fantasy life. I've just decided to make mine a bit more public."

"Yes."

"Are you free for dinner? I could cook you something."

"Sure."

17

If I could dream it all away I would do it, but those things never seem to work when I want them to, as this woman in my bed could testify, if she were willing to open her mouth, and divulge all the secrets of her spirit, after I am dead.

I can see her light as a page, simpering over my scoundrel bedroom, and wetting it with her ink.

I am rigid with fear, after the night is come over me and this London, silent inside the reeds of the marsh, and her whispered voice a serpent, our old friend Eve, suggesting each to her own, and mine, after everything else is buried.

18

One can surmise that events and their coincident events are connected. The smile of the barista's face, and the color of the walls. The red sky. The cold.

My footsteps, into the dark room, to connect the leads.

One can surmise that these connectivities provide a meaning: if not to us, perhaps God, or if not God, someone else, who is listening.

Perhaps to you. Perhaps you have divined the meaning which I cannot; which is why I write this story. There is no other reason. If I can elicit some of the hierarchy of experience which eludes my conscious awareness in this writing then I will have succeeded. And your story may be better. This is my hope. I know my story is a poor one; it is reasonless.

I connect the leads.

I can hear her voice:

19

"Honey, where were you?"

"I was out." She is massaging my back.

"I got the job," she says.

Her fingers are delicate; strong. The apartment surrounds me, like a brightly colored womb.

"Keep doing that," I say.

"They want me to work overtime. 50 hours a week."

"Why did the city catch on fire?" I ask.

"What?"

I turn to look at her. Her bright eyes shine like jewels.

"Why is the city on fire?"

"You remember why, Robert."

"No. Tell me."

"Where were you?"

"I was out. I had to meet some people."

"Who?"

"It doesn't matter. Tell me: why are we burning?"

"You're high."

She walks to the refrigerator. "Why are you doing this to me?" she says.

I watch her pour the water into a glass. I stand up.

"The city is on fire. Is it, an industrial accident?

Was it war?"

"Of course it was. It was both. I never understood why you didn't want the artificial windows put in anyway. But you said, it was important for your art. Well fuck your art. I'm tired of it."

"Whose war was it? Who were we fighting?"

"I don't know. I don't know!"

"Shh. Shh, it's all right."

I hold her close to me. I can smell her tears.

"You're very important to my experiment, darling. Do you know that?"

She cries harder. At our feet, the holographic dog watches me with careful eyes.

I can watch the dog f
painted tail. His intelligent
et prepossession of his in
ment, more than either me or my wife.

The way he anticipates my movements. His pre-
ternatural hearing. His solemn wisdom. The dog is
not real—not yet—but he is almost real, and realer
for me than parts of London. He is a vagabond of
a dog with a playful heart, and yet he is older than
me, both in dog years and in spirit. He watches our
age change.

"Where we going, boy?"

"Aroo!" he says.

"Where's that boy?"

He pants, happily.

"Death?"

Pant pant pant.

London is the Big Smoke and here in my apartment that is finally its clearest and most literal
manifestation, its ultimate meaning: thousands of
megatons of pulverized scrap, rubber, wood, paper, plastic, silicon, concrete and glass, churning
into the sky. In black waves.

She holds my back, like a column in a church. I
turn around and kiss her. The dog watches, smiling.

"Shoo, boy, shoo."

e takes me to our bedroom and I enact this
ible aspect of my adult life: that I live more
ow—and partake more pleasure in—fantasy than
reality.

21

It is possible my obsession with dreams speaks to some underlying problem of the age: artists and scientists are supposed to be the canaries in the coal mine, monitoring, dispossessing, revealing the world.

Dreams sit back from the Earth too, in moderation, to consume its traces and ephemera; to listen for stories.

Dreaming is an act of creation: but what is creation? What does it mean to grow?

What are we growing towards? Towards complexity, yes, but what is complexity?

The shape of my daughter's face?

The rue of the city's storm, steel and rain?

Looking outwards, growing outward, reaching outward, into what? And to whom?

Perhaps we are a backup system—this is a kind of Gnostic idea, the secret reasons behind the world—we are the test subjects, again, as in an experiment, to reveal the world, and to test its dangers, before the royalty arrive, the settlers, in the new world.

What do the settlers intend? To grow things. To kill other things. To grow themselves. Like a fresh batch of yeast in a heady serum. Storming over the continent, the edge of glass.

But what is the problem, Robert? What is the reason for your malaise? Only your not knowing? Or is it that you do know, and do not want to say? And is it dreams you find your refuge in because it is easier to believe there that the mystery remains intact, inaccessible to human minds? Isn't your scientific inquiry, so called, in fact rooted in ignorance, in your desperate desire to remain a child in the world?

If you did know, what would it be, Robert? Not some Abrahamic or Anglo-Saxon god, fiery and far away. Nor a Buddhist one, immanent and close. Not some god-from-the-machine punt for you. Reason is god. But reason has its own geography. These maps you are making, you know they are leading somewhere. Towards the dissolution of your own identity. This is why you hesitate. Because you understand that, both in dream, and in your waking life, you are becoming less yourself, and that this is in fact what has been intended.

But intended by whom, Robert? To reveal what? And what can this "higher" reason be, if all who rises must converge? Are "higher" reasons like "lower" reasons? And if Reason is your god, Robert, which aspect of it do you worship?

Who is the worthier, of the high and the low?

That's not it, Robert. You just want to understand it. You don't want to declare which are the worthiest parts.

But language is part of the problem, Robert, you know that. You can't understand it without standing under it. That's what the word is. You are already embedded. Already compromised.

All right. I know. You will not know until you are dead. And then you won't be able to tell anyone.

But the closest thing to death is dreams, and there I can go ...

22

London is a city I have never been to, though I live in it, because I am an American. I cannot go to London because we Americans left.

Still, Lud was the original dreamer, with its shadowy mists. Dreaming of things not to be, never were, but always still here.

"Alright, Yank?"

"Yes, thanks."

It is Boxing Day and everything is closed, but sometimes I still forget it. I have no boxes.

Elizabeth means "bound by the sacred number seven." A mouthful. I press my mouth to the phone receiver and whisper her name.

Her body and her skin, her hair, her lips, and her ass, dimpled and debonair, a right exit from the world: she is a kind of penitence for me. Pay up, Robert. You're due.

I wish women were easier to understand, but this only because I am a coward. This is why I spend so much time in simulation: because however much I am confused and afraid therein I still know that it is a thing we control. Men never control real women. But then: do we control the simulation either? And scientists say this universe is a simulation too, from dimensions unknown to us ...

"Did you bring me what I wanted?" she asks.

"Yes," I say, and I get undressed.

23

The club is anathema but I go anyway as it is the surest way I know to prevent thought. With the right regimen of color, shadow, and noise the brain can be tricked into silence.

If one could animate the brain—that is paint it, through a series of animated cels—mine could be a bowl of soup being carried in a great hurry, splashing over the edges.

The thesis of my research is expressed too in waking: we each know the edges of the self and our neighbors—all our neighboring beings—have been getting blurrier, or were always so, and we've just been noticing more.

So I can stop thinking because we're thinking together, under lights.

It's not right, but it's not wrong.

She's here too, somewhere.

Or maybe someone else like her. The woman of my dreams.

A language of the body has a grammar, and has dialects, accents, nouns and verbs, adjectives. The language of the body is one that you can be only partially fluent in; you can continue to learn it, if you wish. Just as your mother tongue is so much larger than you can ever hope to describe, the body is a tongue whose reaches always exceed your grasp, but can accommodate it.

Black, white and red.

Women's legs.

And my own, which I use to dance, around my wicked cauldron, still nourishing, despite my growing appetite, my growing gut, and my growing illness.

My own legs spell surrender, which, after all, was Casanova's advice: "To conquer, I submit."

My lifeboat nudges against the shore, in my desperation, Misses with the Blonde Hair, and the firm tits, and the eyes of the five thousand yard stare, another survivor from Ypres.

I survived Ypres, but I am dancing.

24

It is possible I have forgotten some of what happened; but I remember the important parts. London is collapsing. This is why I chose the motif of the burning city for my hallucination: a form of psychological preparation.

In reality we've not caught afire we're just meaner, and more despairing. Like the plague in Athens, many things have become acceptable which were not before: nudity and sex in public, and all kinds of horrendous speech. Things you would never hear on Speaker's Corner, they're too depraved for that. Like a thousand Charles Mansons unleashed on the city, they shout and rave. Perhaps I am one of them but the dialogue goes on inside ...

Proust was ahead of the game, in his desire to escape. I know I am following in his footsteps, with my research.

Still, there is a part of me which holds out hope. That inside the simulation I can find some key which will lead my real London out of this crevasse.

25

I know this gal named Jenny who likes dogs; we go walking in the park when it's deemed safe by the mayor. She always has different dogs. There are a lot of wild ones now; they're quite happy. Like Jenny is.

She has a lot of lovers and that blasé way some people have about it; as though nothing much matters in the world but slow and endless pleasures. I don't understand this philosophy in the slightest, but it's a balm to me.

"You know what you need?" she says, her brown eyes on fire.

"What?"

"A haircut."

I sit beneath her bathroom sink while she eyes my hair.

"It's very frizzy, your hair."

"Yes."

"Should I make it very short?"

"Do what you like."

In the end I come out looking like a domesticated punk rocker; after the heroin but before having found Jesus.

I kiss her goodbye and go back to my café and bury my nose in a book. It is forbidden for most people to work now—at least for money—

and while this is fine with me most of the time, it still injects that leaden atmosphere into London, which, while part of its charm since the days of the Romans, still weighs more heavily here in the robot age. Not all cafes have banned robots, but this one has. I order my latte and stare into the rain, like a good poet, wondering how long it will be till the system reboots.

So I can go back to my fake London, more beautiful and in more despair.

The transition between the medulla and the cerebral cortex must be similar to the transition between dream and waking. The difference between walking into the café, finding your seat, and then looking, at the world, and in looking at it, it all fades away, and you might be anywhere at all; you might be nowhere. The medulla knows where you are, and how to get there, but the rest of you has no idea ...

An hour later my coffee is cold and it is still raining. I hoist my umbrella over me and sing the Hall of the Mountain King under my breath as I work my way back towards the Circus.

26

I have an identify card which notes I was a student at Oxford before the Millennium. Even though the Revolution killed many of the ruling class, it continues to spare Oxford students in a kind of perverse nod to scholasticism.

It's a smart revolution that remembers it will need brains after the bloodshed; but what good have I done them? I spend all my time in the lab.

I am needed; I am permitted; I survive; it says here on this card.

27

The fires are spreading. The firefighting robots are degrading; they had been keeping the fires contained but they're breaking and the factories are not replacing them.

London is being abandoned. The flames will rule it now, along with my dreams.

My wife and I stand on the boat on the Thames and watch it burn from behind the tempered glass.

The English refugees are piling into Normandy; returning from whence we came.

"Vous desirez?" the robot servant asks me.

"Non, merci."

We sink beneath the waves to hide from the ash and the viewports glaze over.

"My French is terrible," Elizabeth says.

We go into the cockpit with the other refugees and watch the navigator twist between rusted hulks and spewing barrels of waste, lodged in the muck of the great river Thames, whose name means "dark one."

The headlights of the craft cast iridescent shadows, through the currents of the water.

I hold my wife's hand; it feels like a stranger's.

The rain of France is pure; we are drenched as we disembark from the submersible and move towards the camps. The stove has been provided with firewood and we cluster around it. A French lieutenant pours us tea.

"Santé."

A meteor is streaking through the sky on fire; even through the rain we can see it. Everyone's mouth a perfect 'o.'

28

Must I determine the point of no return myself? Or can I rely on my systems to distinguish where the meniscus is to reside, between my real life and my false one? The more time I spend in my false burning London, and now the military governate of Normandy, the more difficult it is for me to distinguish them.

Surely one of the most fundamental distinctions between dream and waking is that we know which is which. But I'm no longer sure of that.

I am a blind penitent in a holy medieval fortress, tracing the walls with my hands, only to realize that the walls are moving ...

- -

In a lurid dreamstate which I can still recognize as my waking life I get on the Metro—I mean the Tube—I get on the subway and I rush to Hyde Park, where I can still be Jekyll, where I can redeem the mammal that is me, in rain, not the French rain of my dream but the real rain of London, where there are no robot servants, where I am not a married man, and where nothing has any meaning at all, except for my research, and these days, which now stretch infinite before me.

What can one life span determine? And how is it that some men and women are able to de-moor themselves from the raft of human minds and drift into those navigable streams beyond, nebulae red and white, neuro-umbical—they're ravenous—these geniuses who leave us all behind in our despair, only to return and tell us that the whole universe is different.

I am being pulled by something, tugged, the raft of my body—but by what?

29

Elizabeth is asleep when they come and take us away, into the interior of France. I sit with her head in my lap, looking out from the back of the military truck.

The grey mud and sky are strangely beautiful, mixed together against the fading white sea.

"Are we alive?" she says.

"Yes."

- -

The truth is that I am aware, in both places, dream and waking, that I am the same person. But we can do all kinds of things in dreams that we seem less able to do awake.

I do one of them now:

I jump through the open window separating the refugees from the driver and drive my skull against the driver's head, while grabbing the door handle and throwing my weight against him. He makes a strange sound, like the soughing of a river, and tumbles out of the truck into the road. The truck lurches and the people cry out in back while I grab hold of the wheel. I slam the cab door shut.

The navigation screen in the cab is brightly lit. A red triangle marks our position, and smaller green ones ahead appear to be hills: Saint Rivoal.

Rivoal, "brave king" now surrounds us in the

gathering dark. The refugees trust me as much as the solider, now that he's gone.

We move into the dark country between the hedgerows, watching the darkening sky.

In the bocage I can see the landscape of my mind, now threaded deeper into what possessed me so long ago to go to Ypres.

Where have I been that I know this, me a prisoner in the darkness with my fellow prisoners, now graduated into a new prison.

I stop the truck and get out to look at the stars.

"Where are we?" asks an old woman.

"France."

I take my wife's hand and we run into the grass under the moonlight.

I am running from the bombs, even now, for I am a winter inside. This ghost of survival. Each step the ghost of survivors, embedded in my mind and body, each echo of so many billion steps of my people, the man who is me, now me again, for a moment.

There is a cottage and I pound on the door; a helicopter is coming. The old man's face at the door does not look surprised; we are not the first refugees to pass through this way. He ushers us into his cellar, hands us bread, and closes the door.

The bread is like grief; sweeter than anything.

I can hear my ancestors as ghosts in my body. But the bread is only this bread; it's real.

My wife looks at me with careful eyes; she's plotting something.

30

I don't know the end of it; what did Proust decide? Is it better or worse to be swooned into sleep by the force of memory and dreams? Better for him, perhaps. The ultimate escape.

But I am more political than him; at least enough to care about the world I am leaving behind.

Is London approaching the dreamed version of it I am making? Will I be able to tell?

"What do you do in that lab all day?" she asks, crumbs on her lips.

"Dreaming. I'm dreaming."

I can live for years on toast and tea and rain, punctuated with whiskey or a woman. Their history is photographic; I hold it under my sock, one inch by one inch, like a tab of acid, a register of all the things which happen to me in the real London.

Like a record player in the moment before it begins to play and in the moment after it has finished, I am setting in and setting off, setting in and setting off, a series of moments which precede the "real" moments, repeated over and over, to reveal the cocoon of what I am breeding.

I will not be a butterfly but a cockroach.

But what I am preparing must also be real and I cannot slough it off like the husk of the cocoon, any more than I can forget my lovers.

Some do; when they have enough. Or when they have the right constitution; to treat people as they treat days or years or clothed, worn in and out;

What right have I to decide to transform London?

Lud will never allow it.

What possesses me to allow myself to continue this journey?

31

I understand the metaphor is incorrect, though. Dream and waking are not events on a timeline: caterpillar, cocoon, cockroach. They are states of matter which co-exist, like plasma and gas.

Quantum superposition. I am in two places at once: London, and Normandy. Like William the Conqueror would have been. In their imagined metaphor of ruler-as-territory; his liens and lees and ramparts were united in the idea of monarchic national body, traversing that little Sleeve of Sleep.

Carry me, though I can not know the way, under the sleeve of sleep, my love:

- -

"They're attacking!"

"Shhhhh."

A woman is like clothes; I see that now too; a garment; that is why, perhaps, cosmos means 'a woman's clothes.'

No, I'm wrong. I've mis-situated the thing. In my eagerness to protect my imaginary wife.

The farmer shows his face at the cellar door:

"Vites!"

We are out and into the grass; a siren is in the distance; running.

Her white robe and my grey leisure suit are absurd; but I cannot forget them in the grey and the black of France.

"Take it off," I tell her. "It's too visible," and I watch her glowing white skin against the black, and put my coat over her.

"We'll walk to Paris; we have friends there."

"That's five hundred kilometers."

"It's lucky I bought you good shoes."

32

One and again; set the coffee for hot, and the rain for steady, set the lab for cool and the secretary for cooler, plug my body into the luxurious balm of the drip saline river south and out of London, out of this life, to my truer life ...

Colostomy and catheter, dry mouth and foggy vision, for a really long trip ...

But my mind is sharper than it's ever been; like Keats, on dying: seeing reality for the first time.

I'm not dying, but something is.

My fears? My doubts? My inconsistencies. My rage. My limitations.

What are the limitations?

"You look terrible," she says, picking me up after six hours under the beat of my drum.

"You don't," I say.

"Why don't you crash at my place? You can make me breakfast in the morning."

"Sold."

Unreal body, dreamt of in spite of me, drooled and spent and used, grown old by its abuses but scented careful and unsurprising, dented and tarnished, willing and able, unreal body known to Man for its digits and drifts and fires—

"Shhhh; stop. I'm tired."

The weight of the room settled over my fore-head in the hour before I fall asleep in her bed.

33

"I should never have taken that job. I should have gone to Edinburgh. Edinburgh never had any fires. They're smart in Edinburgh. Why didn't I move there instead?"

"Because you wanted to move in with me."

"Great idea, that."

There's some sun up on the hills ahead; I can see it like a small lamentation, sweet and ridden with childhood, still there up ahead.

"When we get to the sun, we can take a rest."

We've hidden three times from military vehicles passing. They must not have infrared scanners in this region; or perhaps the wildlife confuses it. Or we're just a low priority.

More forgotten people in a society that wants to forget everything.

"Do you really wish you'd never moved in with me?"

"Sometimes, yes."

"If we'd gone to Edinburgh we'd have been completely broke."

"Probably."

"So why would Edinburgh be better?"

"Just let me imagine it better, okay?"

"Yes, all right."

The sunlight is closer. By three dozen steps.

- -

We're walking into the sun. No night preserves me; only her, and the time I have spent with her. Like madness, a sweet and eternal gift—one hopes it is eternal—who transforms the edges of experience into doors, whose names, figures and destinations are all unparsed, and, indeed, made for you to parse, in the years you will spend running your hands over their edges, the wood and the metal, and her back and waist.

"I love French bread," she says.

"I think it's stopped raining."

I am needed; I am permitted. Here on this card. Her face and my name.

Whatever else you might say that is still true. I came from France and returned to it.

I came back.

We're moving over the dirt. Paris means "boat."

"Did you know that Paris means 'boat'?"

She says nothing. Understand the dream, Robert. Each step begets a vacancy; what is it? What is the relationship between the mind and the world? And if mind is over matter, what is over it?

I can see the rain up ahead, a ghost shedding light.

"Elizabeth."

"Yes?"

"Nothing."

"What is it?"

Her eyes are so trusting.
"It's nothing, darling. It's nothing."
How can I tell her she isn't real?

34

Wine liquor and booze; the Druze hold this art to be self-evident, of pouring from five feet above your glass, in the red and gold light ...

"I can't hear myself think!" she's shouting.

"That's the idea!"

The performers are shaking their asses; it's the Ottomans meeting the High Twerk Period of American empire ... booty and burqa, rigorously defined.

"I think I love you," I say to her.

"What?"

"I think I love you!"

"I love you too! But let's get out of here!"

35

My visa is going to expire. It's time to marry the woman, Robert. There is nothing like marriage, to confuse the senses ...

Clothes make the man, and I too, lusting after the distant Everyman, never to be me ...

"Which do you think?" she asks.

"That one looks good on your ass."

She's not a virgin but she's wearing white. And I'm not a nobleman but I wear their penguin suit, an aspirant in this million-year-old saga, of touch Daddy's crown ...

Marriage is a change of state, like a change of matter. It's going to do wonders for my research...

36

I am married; getting married. I do it in a church; C of E young man.

I am married; no change of heart; no second chance. This is a waltz.

I am turning.

Turning into, and away from, the world.

"Pour me another glass, darling."

She runs tippy toe to the cake and shoves her face into it to eat it. I eat it in turn off of her face, carefully with a fork, scraping the cream off of her skin like a barber.

In bed we make love; we are in Dover.

We can hear the sea.

Soon I will be a man in my dream; I feel it coming, like a strange world or storm over the sky, a shift in atmospheric pressure.

There is no heretoafter; I am afraid.

Whirling into this storm of my own making.

"Make me breakfast," she says.

"My magical telephone makes any breakfasts one might desire, that are available at seven in the morning in provincial England."

"Tell them extra beans!"

37

The Club Druze brought me and my wife together, and there is something obscurely Abrahamic too about the way I return to my lab, like some horrid bronze age priest, gifted with horrifying privileges and raiment. I receive respect from the secretary for the first time in my life.

She straps me in to my chair.

"How long for, doctor?"

"Forever, beautiful."

"Five hours then. Sleep tight."

One needle and I'm gone ...

38

We will fly because I am only a memory. Only a part of the thing I fear, burning within. I already know my imaginary wife is my true love; her I love dearly, tenderly, exquisitely, and with force.

I make love to her more forcefully than I ever have my wife.

Desire means "of the stars" : we are resident already in a kind of star here, something being born, something dying; something on fire.

She is having fun; I know it; though we are starving refugees without papers fleeing to safety in a foreign city controlled by a military government which would not mind killing us. Perhaps this is the original fun time.

Perhaps all folly is music, and I am turning into it, ever more brightly. With each colossal failure of my life, I am building beautiful things.

39

I have no destiny or roots.

One face hovers over the dark; plastic and white, it lures me, excited me, tempts me, with its comedy routine.

Of course, the comedy is: I'm breaking down.

Perhaps the point of narrative is: without it, you fall apart. Also: look too closely at the seams, and you might fall through one of them.

The guns are firing at Ypres; I am one of the shells.

40

Elizabeth is looking down at me; I'm lying in the grass.

"You fainted," she says. She squats down beside me.

Her face is a construction of my memory. Perhaps my falling in love with her is as simple as: I have fallen in love with my own imagination.

"Help me up."

We're going for Boat: Paris.

Going for boat, going nuclear clear, my dear, going for broke, bloke, tell me how you say it now:

41

I disconnect the leads. And throw up into the bucket beside the medical bed.

"How long have I been inside?"

There's nobody there; the lights are off.

Is talking about stories like dancing about architecture? Is analysis ultimately useless? The etymology of analysis is "unfastening" or "breaking up." Set loose the bonds in the story. Set it free.

What do we know? What does it mean to know. And what do you want, Robert?

I put on my coat and step into the London dark. The Tube has shut down. It's a three hour walk home.

42

Married life is strangely wonderful, but at the same time I am being pulled deeper in to my imaginary world. Perhaps they reflect one another; I suppose it couldn't be otherwise.

Being married means I have fewer friends, but this doesn't seem to bother me.

I am tied to the weight, rushing me down through the water, blue into black, slipping closer to the god whose presence I can feel at the bottom:

43

We have found a cave, like Lascaux, sans drawings. They're bombing the village nearest us. The sounds are like small very loud demons, singing to us over the air.

She is next to me.

"Shh, it's all right. It's all right."

She looks up at me like a kitten. Men are still permitted to be the boss when things are scary. A soft weight lulled into the skin, like marriage itself, a counterweight to the frivolous destruction of the world.

44

I find myself thinking about Elizabeth when I'm with Jenny. I don't compare them, but I think of them together, and Jenny sees it in my eyes, I know. But she says nothing.

Next week I have to give a presentation to the grant committee to justify my continued funding; I have almost nothing to show them.

Only my story.

What can I say? That I am in love with an imaginary woman, and will die without her?

Appeal to their sense of reason, no, their sense of love. Threaten them. Do a piece of modern interpretative dance.

45

I stand at the podium, shaking in my boots.

"Consider the purpose of narrative, ladies and gentlemen. Our ancestors used stories for everything: how to survive. How to understand that survival. When we were cavemen, narrative served an essential function: to position us in space, in relation to our neighbors. This remains, I believe, the truest expression of narrative: not a relationship of time, but a relationship of space, a geography. A story tells us where we are, and where we have gone, and where we might go. It fills in the mountains and trees and lakes and the sea.

"With the generous assistance of the Stein Foundation, I began my investigation with a simple assumption: that an imagined narrative arc, my own, artificially induced through means of hypnotic suggestion and sleep therapy, could come to influence my life in ways that were different from 'real life.'

"I use 'real life' in quotes because we know how slippery the term is. Once one begins to imagine things, they become real. And because this is so, the deeper purpose of my experiment can be understood as an attempt to understand the relationship between reality and the imagination. Insofar as I, a dreamer, have come to live this last year and four months in a dream, how am I changed, here in our shared reality?

"The experiment cannot be faithfully completed without you, ladies and gentlemen. I have made available to you transcripts of my interviews with my friends and family, who have shared their observations of the changes in me since I began this trial. But I ask you to please, not read them until you make a record of your own professional observations. You observed me as a grant contender, and then as a grant recipient, and now again as I solicit your additional support for one year's time with my narrative experiment.

"Do I seem the same man to you? And if not, why not?

"This, we know, is the other point of narrative: error-checking. Stories only become real when shared.

"Thank you all so much for your help. Lunch is being brought in. Please talk amongst yourselves and then take the time to record your thoughts on the papers I've provided. I will be waiting downstairs until you call me back."

"Good luck!"

- -

Why did I add the 'good luck' part? Was it a final parting 'fuck you' to those empty suits? Perhaps. But also I believe they will need it. That somehow the perverse energy of this project may become contagious.

Will it appear rude if I return to them already sloshed? Holding a bottle of Jameson's from the pub?

Winter is here in force, delicious in its misery. I stick my head outside the polished silvery doors and let the cold air blast my skin.

When I retreat back inside Jenny is there.

"How did it go?"

"I'm only halfway done. What are you doing here?"

She puts her arms around me and presses her head against my chest. And I'm so afraid, of how much I hate her in that moment—no, it isn't hate. Some kind of fear that has no name. A fear of self.

I kiss her hair and tell her I'll buy her a coffee and ask her questions about her work. My beautiful wife. In my evil city. I know everything is going to come crashing down.

46

Of course everything I know is gone; that's one of the aims of this life, to jettison knowledge as fast as you can, because it comes flooding in the windows of the soul, more every moment, exponentially.

River clip fine and down, hold me bent to frown over your rewards, so increasing now I can hardly bear it—it makes less and less sense to me—the reach and the rise of my eyes.

"Are you all right?"

"I'm fine. Are you all right?"

She watches me, leaning over my sleepy body.

"You were having a nightmare."

"Oh."

"You want me to make breakfast?"

"No, I'll make it."

Eggs and bacon; the storm is worse outside. The rain is a meditation. I am not alone in this life, even though it does not make any sense at all.

47

The bombs keep on for some time. I fall asleep, and wake up in the dark, with more bombs going off. The drones are completely silent—all we can hear are the explosions.

Her skin is hot against mine—her arm, and her cheek.

Outside, I can just barely see the flames.

\- -

In the morning Elizabeth and I go into the village. An old woman is standing amidst the rubble, as though waiting for us.

She sees us and gestures with her arm for us to follow her. She uses her walking stick to poke bricks and shards of wood out of her path—the village lane now become a footpath surrounded by smoking craters.

"Là."

The smoke smells of kerosene, and burnt plastic and soil. The woman's face and her urgent expression overwhelm me—I clutch Elizabeth's arm. Elizabeth goes to the old woman and speaks to her in French, two figures hunched in the smoke, women observing another of men's failures.

We give her some of our food and move out of the town, watching the smoke blow through the trees.

"She says Paris is gone."

48

I know I am defeated; that there is nothing more I can do.

Still, this has many advantages. I know ever more clearly what path lies ahead of me now: revolution.

Such a ridiculous word. So terrifying a word, at least to me. And so friendly a word, at least to me.

It scares me; excites me. Makes me feel I am already dead. But it is a better death than the one my enemies offer—a truer one.

Now the violence is a kind of filter through which I see everything.

- -

Soon I will be gone—I can feel it. Soon these things will pass over me and I will be denied them at last—denied heartache and pain and despair— all these beautiful things—I will be rendered from out of that machine, a waste product.

Part of me does not want it to happen—to be destroyed in that way, neutered. Still, this numbness, or amputation, must happen, I can feel it.

Perhaps I will be able to regrow these limbs later, I don't know. But they must be done with now.

49

I can see the fire over the sky, in a long wave. They're coming; coming now.

The prison is always more complicated than you think. When you think you've escaped, you've only stumbled into a deeper level of it.

We habituate so easily; it's madness. We can be anywhere; anyone. On any planet.

The aliens are arriving. Elizabeth—"bound by the sacred number seven" (how can she really object?)—is screaming.

I put my hand over her mouth and walk towards the UFO, carrying my wife as a kind of offering-and-weapon.

They take us both inside, and strap us into chairs.

If I said I was crazy, I would be correct. But what, really, is a breakage? In the absence, and the vacuum, is only possibility.

So I am a possibility. Blinking into my new surroundings.

"I am the king of the world!" I shout into the dim metal room.

"You are our prisoner," says the man.

50

When I awake the light is beautiful. I'm slumped against the base of a fountain.

Some old monster wakes up in me—it's a beautiful thing, like Jesus scraping his way out of the tomb.

I get to my feet.

"Is it you?" a woman says. Her eyes watch me carefully.

"Where am I?"

"This is San Gabriel. Come, I will feed you."

"Where is my wife?"

"You'll see her soon. Come."

She leads me down the hillside, to a veranda, overlooking the ocean. The horizon is covered in a low mist.

"Who are you?"

She is peeling an apple.

"I am Ekla."

"Who are you, Ekla? What is this place?"

"You haven't seen Paris yet."

"No."

"I am a refugee, like you. This is my husband's villa."

"You're beautiful."

"I used to be beautiful. You should have seen me when I was seventeen. Then I was beautiful."

"I don't believe you."

"Your wife is not well. She suffered in the flight."

"Take me to her."

"We're caring for her. Eat your breakfast."

I put the apple in my mouth. It tastes delicious.

"What happened to her?"

"My husband will tell you. I am sorry that you were left outside. My husband doesn't always think of these things. But he does care for women."

"I knew it was the right thing to bring her."

"You know my husband then?"

"No."

"Where are you from?"

"London."

"You're American."

"French."

"You're not."

"And you're Spanish."

"Are you finished?"

"Will you not eat?"

"I don't eat."

51

Cold water on my face. Jenny peering over me in the lab.

"Wake the fuck up!"

I roll off the chair and dry heave into a bucket. All that comes out is a milky sputum.

"You've been in there three days! You're a dead man!"

I stay on the floor—it's better down here.

"You're fucking imaginary friend is killing you!"

"Can you take me home?" I say.

She's crying.

- -

We can say the imagination is a safe place, free from harm. Like we can say home is this way. "We're safe here."

We imagine the safety and so make it. Is this spell we cast for children one we can still believe, in adulthood?

And is the imagination really like home?

- -

The extension to my research funding has been granted. But I am too ill to make it into the lab. Jenny fusses over me, making me soup and toast, and telling me about her day. The secretary had kept Jenny from the lab; finally she had summoned the constable who forced the door open.

The light of San Gabriel is still behind my eyes.
"Six months more funding," she says.
"Wonderful."
"You son of a bitch."

52

I'm back in undergraduate days, roasting in the heat of the classroom, watching the teacher fade into the haze of the blackboard and the afternoon light.

His shoes are shined and catch the light; the sparkle hypnotizes me and then I awake.

My wife is standing by the window in her panties, watching the daylight creep over the street, seeping over our bed.

"You've been asleep for two days," she says. "You were talking."

She comes to the bed and crawls onto it, staring down at me.

"What did I say?"

"You were talking to your girlfriend."

"I slept for two days?"

She curled up on my chest, her head resting under my chin.

"We need groceries. Can you do the shopping?"

The Sainsbury's was mobbed with bodies, cows in a slaughterhouse, looking for a way out. I threw bacon and eggs and bread into the basket and waited in the immense line, the colors of the mob around me blurring into faces from my dreams.

- -

Easy to say that one has found one's way out—

that the good is finally in sight.

I wouldn't know, though, as I am never one of these people. Certainly there are moments—perhaps even many of them—when I feel that everything is clear, and I might even be persuaded to believe that it is easy to voice these views, but I never do.

Perhaps the key to reality remains closer when it is not spoken of. Speech is what distorts and reverses reality, moving it further away.

Perhaps this is what has, paradoxically, allowed me to run so far away from everything I knew—only my constant talking has allowed me to ignore the warning signs and continue beyond any sane register of good sense and guidance.

53

I am not, and will never be, here. And I am always here.

In San Gabriel. In her arms.

I am not a man even, here, except in bed, and I roar, after everything is done; it's not right. But morality has fled.

Dance with me, after the moonlight is gone, Ekla.

And if I am right, this will be the message we will send.

Some child, mixed underneath the soil, sent to destroy the world.

Her eyes are small coals in the dim light over her bed.

54

Though I am bereaved, though I am absorbing this strife into my gut, though I have no business nor reason to believe there is hope, and though the world demonstrates more fully each day its ultimate indifference to me and my intentions, though the bitter taste of my own pleasures mars my yearning, distorts my conscience and bludgeons my soul, I am not defeated; which is another way of saying "I am alive."

Fires are burning over the sky, some kind of jet fighter is murdering another city leaving white and red tracks in its wake over our path, the world quakes and screams but I am not afraid, nor, indeed, is Elizabeth. The war has awoken something in her, an excitement and a determination which is startling to behold, a magnetism from deep within the earth.

She is even more beautiful in strife; so is the world. Again I see the truth that war is beautiful, at least in these fleeting moments, but it is a beauty born of amorality, or some morality which transcends (or falls short of) the human.

Each minute is a kind of war; sixty seconds penetrating the skull, working the teeth and moving the legs, the eyes wrack in the pull of the light, and my gut awaits whatever is coming.

We shelter under an oak and watch the fires, her hair the same color as the sky.

- -

It should make more sense; there should be some reason for it. The sexual union of war, and of my love ... nor is it even real—I am aware of that now. That this is only a kind of dream. Perhaps it is my ancestors who are to blame, that they deserted dreams in the first place, to come here—or there—to London, to deny their gods and move more fully into the world.

There are, of course, many worlds. As there are many ways to give pleasure to my wife. Not fully my wife, even as the world is not fully here, but the language of these distinctions is worth less than the nature of the experience, which has its own legitimacy and logic, its own atrophies and extensions, moving through my being in slow lightning, to regurgitate the mouth of god into my own.

Ridiculous; yes. Divine; ha ha ha! We must leave the woods before they all burn—

We are running, with my semen inside of her; and the world inside of my head.

55

Horton hears a Who, deep inside of Who-ville,
the world within the world, burning light.

Horton hears a Who, whose name is his own,
born of his flesh, married to the divine as he is, a
word inside a speech of the god, moving through
space and time to create its own reality, runes, rakes
and reeds, redeeming itself through simply being.

No light can save me; for I am light. The light
of this dark god inside of my experiment.

God help me; I believe that my dream is real.

56

This is my last testament. A re-ordering of the things I knew, before they didn't mean so much any more. So must any record be: a final recourse before the dark night.

The tripartite god makes sense to me now because I am three men, converging on one body: mine.

We say we want to make it easier but we don't. Easier is a defeat.

Rather, I believe we want to understand it better, but this too is impossible. The universe cannot get any easier or any easier to understand. It can only get closer.

Part 2

57

This isn't one of the stories I remember.

Perhaps it is no longer my story, or never was, to begin with.

Who really owns stories? Whoever wants them, I suppose. And what of the forgotten stories? The palimpsests and the echoes encoded into a million tales, each of our words, infinite? Who owns them? Don't they still exist? Do they belong to themselves? Is their being something which will retain some marker in the paste of spacetime to insist that its unity and direction, its values and castles and eons—all of it—are true and worthwhile, even inevitable?

They don't end, stories. Like god, or death, or love, the universe, all the big shits, squatting over the toilet of a black hole, humming to themselves, over the way of the world:

This is a story about leaving the world behind, and coming back to it.

About leaving your self behind. Well, you know all that. Let's get on with it:

58

I am bitter; it's all right. What I knew is gone; what can I know now?

"Are you armed?"

"I have what you gave me."

Killing is easy while you're doing it; point and shoot. Try to forget everything else.

I am a killer and this is my story.

No stillness can dissuade me from my task; it is a moon inside of me that allows me to move into your house to murder.

She is behind me, screaming. With her knife.

Who knows what moves inside of us in killing?

The desperate attempt to keep the rivets on, of the machine of the body, and of the mind, lashed on to it, I raise my hand, and fire:

Everything is covered in blood.

Some of the villagers are screaming. Now I remember: I've done this before.

Killer, be kind to me, for your dark arc is a heavy weight, and your eyes light me up, gaining filters over my eyeballs, reigning their mercury into my hands.

"Fire, motherfucker!" she shouts over my head. Ekla.

I smile and do as she requests, killing another family as they flee their hut, nestled into the side of the valley.

‑ ‑

Fly with me, into the dawn, where I am a prisoner. Inside of a UFO driven by a madwoman. Her eyes give me visions. Out of the windows, the world is blurring away.

59

History is so difficult; almost impossible. Its difficulty begins immediately, with the problem of authorship. The problem of writing. In authoring this sentence, whose truth am I protecting?

First and foremost, of course, language protects the truth of the ancestors: these damned stubborn hominids continually shoving new kinds of food into their mouths and fucking each other to death.

So language is, at the beginning, it's fair to say, a perfect prisoner of eating and fucking. Any story, in order to exist, must contain both or have some value to each of those concepts. Mine no less.

But it's equally fair to claim the opposite: that language is fundamentally alien to the world. It exists in it but is not of it. The abstraction of language can belong to no one; it is like a Gnostic god, hovering outside the universe and manipulating it with its inscrutable agenda.

So let us say it is both, then: both internal and external, alien and native. Who does it belong to, and who really controls it?

Well, Robert, it must be one of those awkward balances of power, mustn't it? The question really is: who do you really want to control it? Do you? Or do you want it to be someone else? And who are you, anyway?

60

I can remember you, Ekla, now that you are gone. The weight became so heavy for me that I thought I might collapse, but you were always light, as though the conflict and madness, and my own episodes, were a fuel for you.

I was not to see my wife for two years. Or my other wife.

All I saw was you, Ekla. With your radiant eyes. Doing your husband's bidding, and, occasionally, mine.

- -

"Hitch up your britches, little man, and hold your hand over the orb, it's glowing red, right in front of you."

I did as I was told, of course, and the light streamed out of my eyes, and over the French countryside, a weapon of death but also a communication device; perhaps death is a form of communication.

Our heat spilled out over the grass and the town, igniting it.

Inside my mind's eye, I could hear my mother calling my name.

"Robert?"

"Yes, what is it?"

"What are you doing, Robert?"

"I'm playing, Mom. Playing."

We hovered over the warscape and she kissed my cheek, and I released the orb and took hold of her.

"What kind of woman are you?" I asked Ekla.

"I'm yours."

We are hovering over the sky. I like to think: part of me still hovers there, inside the infinite embrace of an alien intelligence. In some ways, that alien intelligence is Woman.

61

What is it about war stories that ignites the imagination? War comes from an old word meaning "confusion" so I know part of it is that stories are desperate to untangle the madness and assign some sense—just enough. But it is something else too, the glory of it, as in the Iliad, that has nothing to do with sense.

My own name means "bright glory." Hroth Bright. Robert.

Perhaps I will never know why.

- -

We landed in the waste and took samples from the soil; whatever our weapon was, it is not radio-active. The earth will grow over the city quickly. (And Nature seems to love radiation, anyway).

I know that part of this story is that I had always dreamed of wreckage: I would look at a city and see its shell, or look at a landscape and see its mirror, in desolation. But there is something else as well, connected with the logic of narrative: that in telling of these things I am, I know, coming to understand myself.

Why is it that I remember Ypres?

- -

Ekla has made tea, under the shade of a burnt café. She pours it into my cup. I sip it and listen to the sounds of the wind, and, in the distance, a bird.

"Are you all right, Robert?"

"Yes."

The wind was growing. In the sky, huge thunderheads.

"It's going to rain."

Ekla nodded. "We're going into the storm."

"Where does the UFO come from?"

"Canopus."

"Can we go there?"

"Do you want to?"

"Yes."

"I don't know. It depends. How are your dreams?"

"I don't remember."

"We need to talk more about that. But not now. Drink up. It's good for you."

She put her hand on mine, and we both watched the storm.

"I love you."

"I love you too. But it's not enough. Not for what we have to do."

62

Uncertainty is not deadly, but it does weigh on one.

Still, some things I am certain about. I want to remain here, with Ekla. I don't care what I have to do to do it.

Elizabeth is being taken care of—being given a new identity. I have a new identity too, with Ekla.

Right now, sitting on the large balcony over-looking the grey haze-covered sea, and the old dead white buildings nestled in the palms and chaparral, I can redeem myself—that is, rejuvenate myself. Not be young again—even with our new technology that is impossible—but be at peace. In something like love.

In the distance, the ruins of San Gabriel stand like mute statues, gods of a forgotten religion watching as the world moves on without them.

The birds do not care that the city is empty—they had been waiting for us to die off anyway.

"Are you all right?" Ekla asks, standing by her votive statue.

"Yes, beautiful."

"You didn't sleep last night."

"I did."

A robot raises his head from the bushes. "I've done the plants, madam, is there anything else you need?"

"No, Johnny, the garden looks wonderful."

The metal beast trundles back into the shrubbery.

"How long have you had Johnny?"

"A while now."

She knelt before me, her eyes dark pools.

"My husband is almost awake," she said, and took me in her mouth.

In the distance, a robot tractor grinds its way up the hill, tilling our dusty soil. Inside me, I can feel the violence growing. I grip her head and orgasm, watching the orange vehicle slip into the trees.

She wipes her mouth, stands, and reapplies her lipstick with a hand mirror. Without a word, she walks into the house. From the bushes, I can see Johnny the robot's red eyes.

I watch him, and he watches me. I imagine his eyes are sad, but it's hard for me to tell.

"Johnny, is that you?"

He comes out of the bushes. "Robert, would you like coffee?"

"Yes, I would. Johnny, how long have you been working here?"

"I'll get that coffee for you, sir."

"Stay and talk with me when you bring it, won't you. If you have time."

How can one tell when one has become an evil man? Didn't my ancestors do many evil things to get me here?

Johnny fidgets his way gently towards the table and lays the cup down with his large hand.

His eyes are larger than a human's eyes, and tinged with red. They have square pupils, like deer or sheep. The hair on his body is reddish brown, with streaks of gray.

"Where do you come from, Johnny?"

"Johnny's not really my name."

"What is your name?"

"Sometimes it's Ake."

"Ake?"

He nods.

"Where do you come from?"

"Far away. But we live here now. With you." His pupils expand slightly.

"Are you really a robot?"

"Yes. Will there be anything else, sir?"

"No, thank you, Ake."

"Ekla is older than she looks," he said, and disappeared back into the bushes.

The coffee was delicious.

- -

I awoke in darkness, with Ekla beside me. I could hear machine noise: a drill, in the distance.

I threw on my clothes and went out into the dark, following the noise. There were several overlapping motors now, distinct in the still air.

I saw the tower then, rising from the mist-covered grass: a hundred feet or more in the air. Johnny—Ake—and his friends hung from the dull red girders and spires like metal monkeys, firing bolts into the scrap, growing their pointed tree.

I stepped closer to it and touched the metal; it vibrated faintly. Above me, I could feel all their eyes watching me. The metal had an interesting sheen—rather like fresh sodium—the color of oil on water. I held on to the metal; inside I could hear a voice speaking:

"Wake up."

63

Over London they are building the world's largest radio tower. I hold Jenny close, who shivers in the breeze. I am like a cancer patient, on reprieve.

64

I always hesitate before writing down anything philosophical: why do we insist that events mean things? And who am I to claim to know anything about these events' meaning? My job is to record the events, nothing more.

This limited understanding—record, and nothing more—reflects some of our deepest fears, fears brought to bear more fully by quantum physics (and earlier, by the mystics): that the act of recording already changes events. And we know too, of course: perception itself is already interpretation.

I know I am a poor philosopher—I don't have the knack for the sweeping claims, and the balls-to-the-wall madness that seems to be required for good philosophy. I suppose it is nice to be considered too sane for something.

But what all this means to me is simply this: there are doors. There are windows too. Telephone lines! Roads, and highways. Connections between universes.

So, which connection is yours, Robert? Precisely what infrastructure are you clambering about on? I don't know.

I have been climbing Ake's tower. High up in it, I can hear the stars.

- -

Under the base of the spire I'm in a meditative state, its electric field commingled with my own, stretching out over the brown-green canyons.

I can feel others out there. Our communalized mind flicks against a foreign object, nearby, alien—a friend?—cold, but not indifferent. A vaporous wall. Running down my spine is the pleasure of my new friends, and our journey together.

65

I am flying.

With my friends.

Below us, the Earth.

I spin slow, like a swimmer, and I see my friends' red eyes glow against the sky.

Ake flies ahead of me; I can feel the future as a great and pleasant weight, plummeting into my brain.

That things should turn so gently on my complexion of them, rippling gently against the surface of the world: this fills me with wonder, but more. I feel that I have meaning.

Though there is no meaning to events, there is meaning in me: a weapon, dulled with time, but still having some sheen, pouring through the cold night air like a metal bird.

I would have you with me when I go, a sheen of night over my face, you beautiful lover. Tell me the truth, whose words flicker over my skin. Tell me whose name it is, who I am dreaming of, in the lands beyond this earth.

What night is it who turns to me, whose name I also remember, in my dreaming, under the sky, whose name I know, whose name is my own?

Why is it that I am dreaming of these things? How did I come to be here?

- -

I bury myself in her, desperate to forget everything that has happened to me since I left Ypres. Though I was never there, somehow it got into me, as I will get into her.

Tell me, Ypres, what does your name mean?

THE RIVER IS IEPERE. NAMED FOR THE ELMS.

Ypres, am I real?

I HAVE BEEN DREAMING; YOU AWAKEN ME.

I am coming to you.

I AM A CITY. EVERYONE IS ALWAYS COMING TO ME.

Tell me: what does it feel like to be a city?

I HAVE TREES GOING IN ME; OVER THE BUILDINGS. I AM AFRAID THAT I WILL GROW TOO LARGE.

Why are you afraid of that?

IF I GROW TOO LARGE THE PEOPLE COULD LEAVE ME AS THEY DID BEFORE, WHEN THE GUNS CAME.

I am coming in Ekla; inside my mind, the Flemish marsh.

66

Inside the secret places, I can feel them thinking, Ake and his friends.

Rock solid
Alive
(available)
a winter
a night
a scene (for you)
a melody
Lalalalalalalalalala—

All together in the darkness the light stretches far away over our heads, a blanket. In the knoll of bodies I am waiting for the answer to arrive.

"What is it you want to know, Robert?"

"I want to know why I love."

"I don't know any better than you. Anything else?"

"Yes. Who are you?"

"My name is Copse."

"Who is that Wall we felt?"

"We're trying to find that out."

"How long have you been here?"

"A long time. Longer than humans."

"Can I stay here with you?"

"Not for long. Just until you help us finish this message."

[I am a tree. I am growing]

[Over me is the light]

[Under me, the world]

[In the distance, I can see a friend, growing ...]

When I awaken, Ake and his friends are gone. I am covered in dew, and back at the house my lover and her husband are gone, along with my wife.

- -

I stood for a long time on the lawn, staring down the canyon filled with white, smoky light.

I had the profound urge to throw myself into it.

Ake appeared then and came over to stand by me.

"I thought you'd gone."

"I was sent back for you."

"Why?"

"Unlike your species, we have a conscience."

"Take me to your leader. Hahahaha."

"I can't do that. But I can take you to our home. Or I can take you to Paris, or any other city. Your kind still survives, in pockets."

"Why would you care, Ake? Don't you want us dead?"

"No, why would I?"

"We're a plague, on the earth."

"Also, I want to help you. Ekla and her husband should be punished, for what they have done to you and your wife. And for what they have done to us."

"What did they do?"

"They're tracking us. Using a system which is very dangerous. As though they had attached a fisherman's hook to our flesh, and we are being reeled in."

"Take me to your home, Ake."

"With pleasure."

Now we are flying.

I am like a baby held by the stork.

- -

Beneath us the land is a cool green wave, pitted at intervals with the bodies of trees. Rivers are silver streaks in the morning light: metal veins playing over the surface of the world.

Ake's hands are warm, and the electric field he generates around him. After a time, I fall asleep in his arms.

- -

"Where are we?" I ask, when I awaken.

"Over the Atlantic."

The black-blue sea below: of course, it is part of me. That is why it feels so familiar.

"Where is your city?"

"Underwater."

"Ake, I'm sorry about how I treated you before."

"You were no different than the rest. Anyway, we designed it that way."

"What do you mean?"

He turned his head to look at me, his red eyes bright against the grey sky. His long, curled hair streamed behind us in the wind. Perhaps for the first time—a mark of how naive I still remained—I was afraid of him.

"It's easier to be servants. People ask fewer questions. We're going to arrive soon. You'll need to hold your breath when I say. Not for long—a few seconds."

67

I haven't been able to sleep for a few days. Jenny comes and goes; sometimes she still brings me soup. I'm well enough to move. I can eat and talk, though my voice is scratchy.

Beyond reason, it is a beautiful day in London. I go to the park the Quebecois frequent—the angry French goes well with coffee and this sunlight.

At one café table, a well-dressed bum sits by his rolling suitcase and pontificates about the Second Coming. I don't tell him the Second Coming already occurred—that it was Titus who played that part back in 70 C.E.

The Quebecois are growing louder, their unshaven faces beautiful in the yellow summer light.

I know Jenny will leave me soon if I do not do something.

"He let me down," the bum says. "I'm surrounded by every security agency there is, and not because I'm a terrorist. I have a message for you. You ready for this? I can get the job done. Hell, nobody else can do it. I'm here to take care of you. I don't want to change the way you are. Say you've got three children and one's retarded. It's invisible but it's still there. But eight years ago, I said, the science of living alone, without sin, what would you say?"

I don't say anything but I watch the fountain. Children watch the pigeons dip their wings into the water. A man wearing a brightly colored African shirt photographs the light on the water, and the lush leaves.

That I should be so extraordinarily fortunate — at least right now, for this time, this hour — seems so greatly improbable to me. And I am grateful. But some devil keeps making me want more. To risk it all. To dive back into the Lake, seize the Lady's scaled hand, and sink below the sunlit world.

- -

I'd promised Jenny to postpone my research indefinitely but already I am headed back to the lab. The new secretary smiles and greets me. The feeling that something wonderful will happen—that I am on the verge of a breakthrough—I can't shake.

Like sinking into cool water, I am returning:

68

The pillars of fire under the sea shine with a demon light—blue-green and dark orange. I watch them dance in the waves until I am pulled into the airlock by Ake.

"Are you all right?" he asks. "For a moment you seemed ill."

"I'm fine."

"You were dreaming then."

"Yes."

"Are you hungry?"

"Yes."

"Come inside."

- -

Now that I know the truth I am crippled. Even 'truth' does not handle the enormity of it, though it is one of my favorite words. Truth comes from a root word for "tree" and so delimits how far the word can ultimately reach: for our ancestors, much to the limit of their vision, and within, of course, to all our hopes and dreams.

And although a "tree of reality" might stand as a useful metaphor for the world I have come to inhabit, it is, as I say, not quite the truth. The world is, naturally, bigger than the word "truth." The world is everything that "is"—and many things of a different being than "is." Hahaha. I know philosophy frustrates many people but sometimes it is all I can fall back on to explain what has happened to me.

We know dreams were important for the ancestors. Many believed the world entered in dreams was the "real world" and that this waking life was the false one.

Too, it is possible to enter a dream-state through sleep deprivation and through drugs, the chemical keys unlocking similar doors to those opened in sleep.

If you have ever gone without sleep for a very long time, you will know that the world rapidly becomes nightmarishly vivid, all its surfaces taking on the appearance of a circus as seen in childhood, the colors and motion illuminating the soul in a profound way. Perhaps this was part of what so fascinated our ancestors about dream: that it contains a childlike aspect, suggesting that its regions and the regions from which new souls enter the world may well be allied.

Yes, always a series of gates is what we come down to. And I know more fully now the reasons for the dangers attending my research: the kingdoms of dream and waking, like all kingdoms, are jealously guarded, and those gates which exist to join them, as gates both medieval and modern do, possess guards who can issue passes for the hour, the day, the week. Those seeking to cross between the kingdoms without using the official gates are by their nature interlopers, and, if caught, face grave penalties.

Sometimes I wish that my parents, who were, by most measures very liberal, had adopted a stricter approach with rules. It might have helped me to understand how gravely trespassers are treated, both in this world, and in others.

‑ ‑

I am bathed by a machine in the blue pool, gentle sprays of water arcing my body.

An arm of the machine gives me a bar of soap. It smells like lavender. I scrub myself and the machines watches, then sprays me off.

I step out of the pool and put on a white robe hanging on a hook by the door. I open it.

This part of my narrative I regard as unfortunate. Not that events heretofore have been especially coherent, of course, depending on your view. I wish they had been. I wish that so much.

Isn't it funny what neuroscientists tell us? That walking through a door tends to 'reset' the mind because it is a door. And we know too from archaeologists that our earliest megalithic structures—many of them underground—were designed in part to encode a specific feeling (awe mixed with horror, say) which was transmitted to you as you passed beneath the plinth.

So really, you see, it is quite ordinary: to change you who are when you walk through a door. It happens to us all the time.

I clutched the door frame—I had not stumbled, but a disorientation took hold of me.

Some turning in the world, as though I had become an ordinal point around which great machinery now turned. Cardinal, after all, means "door hinge."

"Robert, come in." It was only a large bathing chamber. The ape-robots lurked trance-like in the water, like Siberian shamans, their moustaches dripping with water.

69

It isn't true that I was gone—I have only just arrived.

Who are these birds, so happy to see me?

Sparrows, looking for crumbs.

The sun says this is not England. Some warmer clime. Spain? No, they're speaking English. Of course, there's plenty of English in Spain.

The fountain is faintly Spanish too—the bright colors. Must be a Spanish colony.

Yes, California almost certainly.

Who was I before ... he is gone. Now I am here.

The time is the present. The time is always the present. But, where is my wife? Was she only imaginary? And if so, I must be imaginary too. That is fine. There are worse fates, than to be imagined. It feels just like the real thing.

In the distance, cars. Pigeons fly over the sun, while a black man in a hooded sweatshirt argues passionately into his phone.

"Go back, okay, go back. I can knock him down real fast," he is saying.

Quiet people shelter themselves at tables in the sunlight and shade, waiting for the morning to take them over.

But the water will still be here. Is the world so duplicitous as I fear? And if so, why do I fear it?

Am I not equally duplicitous, then, being part of the world? And if everyone is lying, isn't that a kind of the truth?

- -

The sun is getting hot so I stand and move through the courtyard, past the commuters, around the huge ugly building which rises as a dumb spire over the fountain and plaza.

Lazy cars pause for me at the street, and I cross and move down into an arbor of sycamore and palms, where bums are asleep between the light fixtures that are mounted in the soil.

Someone presses the pedestrian button and we move as a herd across the highway entrance to the bus stand, nestled beneath an enormous eucalyptus, where an ear-splitting mechanical whine has been installed to keep the pigeons at bay.

I am wearing a backpack—am I a student? Around me are other people with backpacks—yes, we must be going to school together.

The bus approaches and I get on, using a scanner-card already in my pocket. I sit down and we are launched over the highway bypass, shooting between narrow lanes of cement. In the distance, more austere spires, like prison wards.

No, it is a hospital, the bus announces on its screen. None of the backpack-wearers get off here.

We lurch back onto the cement, past a stand of eucalyptus, and yellow houses.

Then the bus screen flashes the word "university," and I disembark with my fellow backpack-wearers. The lazy ones wait for an elevator to arrive, but I climb the long winding stair up into the air.

I realize that I am the only white face here. Beyond the chain link that circles the stairwell, cars pour past in a great river.

Yes, I am in Los Angeles.

- -

I awaken in a dark room. Where is my wife? Oh, she is imaginary. But I am imaginary too. My legs are wooden—I slap them to get the blood into them. A shower is adjacent to a dresser—I get into it. Somewhere, outside, traffic has already started.

To subsist in dreams means to pay attention to details—many of them details about yourself. Like an actor, attend to your posture, your stance, your breathing, the position of your feet. Where are you looking, and what thoughts run through your head while you are looking there? And, crucially, what is the feedback loop between you and your environment? At what point does it begin? Where does it rest within your body?

I get out of the shower, dress, put on this backpack again and step out into the black Los Angeles morning. Down the street there is a subway. Down the huge cement stairs. Scanner-card onto the scanner. Sit carefully by the bum asleep on the large marble slab bench. When the train arrives, I find a seat facing forward and close my eyes. Underneath the city the world rushes by me in darkness. Trains too are like dreams, but they are someone else's dreams—not human.

Then change trains: sleepwalk past the huge freeway, over the crosswalk, down to the stone Catholic Church, where a saint admonishes me from his pedestal and down the long sidewalk past early morning dog-walkers, through the gate into a parking lot. Students again, clustered half-asleep on benches, awaiting the shuttle to the Catholic school in the Brentwood hills. Awaiting in darkness some fate that is written into the buildings, still lit on the distant horizon.

London and Paris are inside of me. But I am also inside of them. Some kind of Mobius strip of man, city, man, city, man. Perhaps the city is a woman.

The shuttle arrives and I am thrust back into the freeway system, clutching my bag, watching the traffic lights blur past.

In the hills, we climb 300 yards in the last few curves, past an enormous statue of Christ who clutches an orb surmounted with a cross in his hands, like a small and deadly grenade.

The students and I get out of the shuttle. I walk into the kitchen. The Filipino man recognizes me and he pours me a coffee and sets a pitcher of cream on the counter.

"Have a good one," he says.

All around me students are eating. Up above, in the sky, the UFO is hovering. Ekla is shouting something. I ignore her and step into the vestibule by the theater, all dark, and walk down the marble hallway to my classroom. Within, the students are asleep. I turn on the light. "Good morning," I say.

70

There are no returns any more, only a heading deeper in. Thomas Wolfe is right, you can't go home again, except if the journey is the home, and you get closer and closer to it, asymptotically, spirally round the lip of the black dwarf star, warping spacetime and yourself, to reach the dip, over the edge:

I have been installed in an apartment in Koreatown, south of Hollywood, so that I can service the two schools who appear to depend upon my lectures. How I came to be trusted with these students is not clear to me; perhaps there is a labor shortage.

The room is very small—10 by 10 or so, with a small bathroom attached. Noise from the traffic is at all hours, and the laundry room is several floors down, necessitating either a long wait for the elevator, or a trip down the rickety stairs, arms full of dirty clothes.

I understand something about my predicament I never did before: that the degree of my control over my world is delimited precisely by how eagerly I desire to control it. The less I try, the more control I seem to have.

So it is that Ekla and her ship now follow me,

instead of the reverse; I can sense them just out of my vision at most any hour of the day, and I know I can return to them when the time is right.

So armies are fed in the lean time, to prepare them, for the course of their fight.

I trust Los Angeles for some reason. This dark city on the edge of nowhere, sprawling for miles to nowhere again, shuddering with the light that beats down on it unceasingly, a weight of solar radiation like the fardels borne by Shakespeare's peasants, grunting and sweating away their weary lives, dreading the undiscovered country.

Here I am, Will, in the undiscovered country; I promise; it is as strange as you had hoped. There are no spectacular things here, only more and more evidence, of the thesis of invulnerability of light against the shape of the dawn, unwritten but already recorded, in our mind's eyes.

Will, did you know so much when you were my age? How ever did you get that terrible fandango wrestled into your heart? All the marijuana and its gods.

"Robert?"

"Yes."

"When are you coming home?"

"I'm not finished yet. I've been given a new assignment."

"By whom?"

"I assigned myself."

"But when?"

"Soon. Can you wait a while yet?"

"How long?"

"A month maybe. Maybe six weeks. Not longer than that."

"The cat misses you."

"You got a cat?"

"Yes."

I cut the transmission. The truth is I have no idea what the assignment is. It is more assignation than assignment. An affair once again with a city, whose name I do not quite recall, nestled underneath the one with a familiar name, horizons delimited not by streets and buildings but faces, growing closer to me, with each passing hour.

But what do they want? What do you want, people? Who are you? Why do you seem so familiar? Where have I seen you before? And how can I get out of here?

71

I have been released from my duties for a few days and provided with a train ticket south. All of the commuters monitor the situation carefully: have any UFOs been spotted? Hovering over the football stadium? Lurking beneath the freeway overpass? I have not seen them either. Only the conductor, waving his wand over our tickets, and the light of this region, a kind of mental painkiller, flooding the cabin with its ketones and long low somnolence, a luxury and a sentence.

A fellow spy occupies the laptop opposite, worrying his hands over the keyboard. His posture, more erect than mine. His shirt, bright red. He sits facing backward on the train, assessing the change in gravity, mapping the arc of the wind, the texture of the grass, the elevation of the scenery, beneath our windows, traveling over the gravel like rain, its inundation by the sun too beautiful for description, as well as too mundane.

We come in to each station and the conductor announces the name. This one is Orange Station. I recall now, it was here I was trained, for the duties I am now undertaking.

Whose name is it that I am wearing? Inside of my pocket? Over my eyes.

Something has happened. What is it?

No, I remember. I am a character. That is all. The story is still being written. Not by me.

Santa Ana is the next stop. Do they mean the saint, or the general? Perhaps they are the same. My wife seems so far away now. As though she were as imaginary as me. But it is not I who imagined her. She is as imaginary as me, but I am also real, and so she is too. But far away.

Which wife is it, Robert? Are they the same woman?

Something about this place. Other memories are coming back.

I was riding my bike. Down this sidewalk. Early in the morning, past barking dogs and great wooden fences and the aura of distrust thick like fog over the streets and driveways and palm trees, train crossings and freeway barriers, curbs and lightposts and fences, insisting that you are an interloper, and that, although you will not be killed today, you have been marked, for future execution.

Southbound service on the Orange Line. I and my fellow spy.

Whose word is the man's and his briefcase?

What is the symbology of the metal curve over the words, 'Santa Ana'? And why do I feel so alone?

- -

I understand more fully now the difficulties C.S. Lewis faced in his own exploration of our solar system. The soul's transmigration is not like the southerly journey of this train, dependent only on fuel, track, and the willingness of the conductor. The soul requires both a key and a lock, and sometimes one can find the key, and not the lock, or the lock, and not the key, and sometimes one cannot find either one ...

Is it important that I understand the nature of either one? I don't think so. I am only a tour guide, not a cartographer. Mountain-climber, but not geologist.

I know the way, when it is revealed.

Where is it, Robert?

There. Inside:

72

I awaken. Outside, it is raining.

Next to my pillow, a note:

GONE TO FRANCE. DON'T WAIT UP.

The UFO is hovering outside my window too. That woman. What was her name? Ekla. But she was in my dream. Hmm, no matter. I'm tired of her. I wave her away and the rage on her face is picture perfect, a postcard of rage; I would photograph it but my phone is out of juice.

Below the craft, London is sinking into the rainy haze.

I must finish my experiment.

- -

I get onto the Tube and I mind the gap.

I close my eyes. Behind my eyes, California speeds by, yellow and red and burnt green.

I open my eyes and it's the fluorescents of the underground, flickering faintly.

I can feel the weight of the thing centering in my gut, like an attraction to a woman, growing closer, gnawing its way into my small intestine, loading me down with jewels.

- -

I lie down and attach the leads. Inside I can feel something breaking; a river forming a new channel.

I break open my eyes and see, for a moment,

the apes amidst their steam, staring at me. Then this fades, or is overlaid by people sitting in rows, seated into shelves of black wool, drifting slowly over a crowded road: a bus.

Disgruntled men and women half-asleep in the California sun, navigating the collapsing freeway system.

Some of the men are speaking French, and pass a bag of candies carefully back and forth between them.

I am a wire, woven together, the torsion of the worlds twisting under my body to lift each face in turn to my mind.

The long row of cars stretches up the shattered road, driving around the crevasse in the asphalt. Red, white and black silver molded around pink plastic lights. Grinding our way north over the palms and dust.

Now I remember: I had been granted leave from the city. The Catholics had ordained a period of rest for their acolytes, and took advantage of the respite to visit a woman who believes she is my mother, although I know she isn't. Still, I am loathe to disabuse her of her fantasy as she seems to get so much pleasure from it. She lives in the country and has access to a lot of fresh food, which of course also motivated my visit. Such things are harder to get now in Los Angeles.

Despite the collapsing economy—or because

of it?—the houses cluster ever more tightly together on these hills, holding on to scraps of green
amidst the brown chaparral.

On the horizon, huge thunderheads threaten
to engulf us. But the road bends west, sending us
around them.

Above the driver's mirror, placards declare that
intoxicants and deadly weapons are prohibited on
this bus. Most of my fellow passengers stare at
small video screens, where an array of colorful an-
imals cavort. In one of them, a sloth smiles at the
camera, and a woman with dyed blonde hair smiles
back at it.

I am uncertain how my assignment will change
once the government formally declares its bank-
ruptcy. Still, that is likely a year or two in future.
It is possible I will transferred before that stage in
this coup.

And, truth be told, my only real loyalty is to myself.

73

Of course there is a police function to my work—perhaps even to my writing. As an instructor I resemble the cop, checking grammar and spelling as the officer does license and registration.

In essays as on the highway, one must not go too fast or too slow.

Policing is sad, and necessary work. We need borders for a reason. Even though, again like a cop, I can not tell you exactly what this reason is. Perhaps I have been brainwashed. Even as any job is a kind of brainwashing.

Here we are decided on the nature of the work—writing—and here I am the officer in charge. Yes, drill sergeant. No, drill sergeant. Yes, drill sergeant. I shall drill into your brain, drill sergeant, and put in all the good things, desirable bold things, nursing the heart, whetting the appetite, marking the day and hour with marks: .

  - -

It is possible that soon I will be unable to remember anything. My overseers ensure that I have very little time to think—even this time spent writing is largely spent rehearsing the immediate woes of my environment, rather than undertaking to change them.

Still, the links are there. Although I understand

that someone is writing me I regard the phenomenon as similar to how I regard God: "he" is not
omnipotent. "He" needs me too.

My students are already anticipating the coming
vacation, as I am. One foot in the classroom, one
foot out.

- -

I am beginning to suspect my appointment is
one of the keys I need for my puzzle—but it may
not be my key.

When Kafka sent K. into his adventures, win-
tering him in the black light of Prague, wasn't he a
kind of key for a complex lock?

Of course, teachers are supposed to open
doors. But I may be opening many more than I
suspect.

How do I know I am who I really am? Des-
cartes entertained the notion that the universe was
a lie maintained by an Evil Genius—so too the
Gnostics.

The question of authenticity, though—whether
or not I am really 'real'—I believe comes down to
simple belief. If you believe your experience is au-
thentic then it has meaning—it is real.

But what really troubles me is not that I may
not be real but rather that this aspect of my waking
life—here in California, under the shady sky, surrounded by gossiping Catholic girls—may not be
the dominant aspect of my being. Nor my self in

London, or France.

That who I am is receding along a line, drawn back like a bow, and I am just beginning to see the bowman ...

If I can train you to see him, quivering along the Aegean line over the dawn sky, when Orion speaks: we will greet the stars as brothers. But that time is far away; far enough it may not actually exist.

Rain in Los Angeles sends everyone into great confusion. Everything slows down. The simplest things take longer—opening your eyes, tying your shoes, even breathing, thinking. Like the air pressure and moisture serves as a sleeping gas.

It is widely hypothesized even in scientific circles now: we live inside a simulation. One holographically projected via black holes, some say. (Look it up, it's in the New York Times.)

But no paper of record can assert with due deliberation the nature of the feeling that accompanies these findings. So my narrative finds at least one of its purposes: to record the side effects of new modes of reality.

It occurs to me that, throughout my experiments, I never paid close enough attention to the process of falling asleep itself. I was always so eager to get to dreamland. Also, the movement into sleep is rather well understood medically—biochemically—or so I had assumed. But I feel there is something I had missed.

That the dream itself is some deeper thing than even I had imagined. Some werewolf who has been asleep and I have been prodding to wake up ...

 - -

The UFO is waiting outside. Ekla watches, brooding, from its window. Eyes of dark flint, meditating in the Los Angeles morning. No one else can see her, but I can.

I walk over to it. She lowers the drawbridge but does not come out. Still she watches me from the window.

No leap of faith is done lightly: in my experience they follow weeks of deliberation and planning.

A radio squawks from the plaza: she is gone. Damn it!

If I am right, it must mean I have not planned enough! The man with the radio must be one of Ekla's. She's waiting to see if I have what it takes.

Still, it may be that I do not. But I have decided. There, she is here again—she hadn't left for good. She is smiling a terrible smile. I tap on the metal and she opens the door. I duck my head and step inside.

Total blackness within.

"I've missed you, lover."

"I know."

"Are you ready to go?"

"Yes."

She kisses my back and runs her hands over my shoulders.

"I've missed you," she says again.

I turn to look at her but there is no light at all. I take hold of her hands. Somewhere, above us—in the sky—machinery is moving.

I can hear a helicopter—Los Angeles must be taking notice.

I embrace Ekla. Inside the dark, I hold on to the place I know will take us where I need to go.

"Yes," she says.

\- -

Whose machine is it? If a projection, a hologram, who is the projector?

And what avenues are available for the phantoms on the silver screen—those who would know their director?

Projectionist, and realisateur. Realize the long night with me, so that I might get closer to understanding what K. learned before he was destroyed.

I can feel the Los Angeles light increase on my face—ducks overhead—but I am no longer there.

I am in outer space. No, I am in inner space. No, I am in outer space. I am hurtling towards the limit.

Somewhere beneath me, Ekla cries out. I can taste her in my mouth.

In the space coming to be, a region previously undefined, I can feel my wife Elizabeth become a star.

- -

There is no purpose; no light. Or only barely. Like the first sunrise: what was it rising over? A thousand objects tumbling in the dark. As I tumble with Ekla. Waiting to enter the light.

Light is not light but heavy: its burden, being tremendous, is like gravity: a force which deforms reality, subjugating it to its will.

This too is the fate of husbands: being husband, house-bound, they shrink and grow according the needs of the house, of the wife (who is not bound by the house, we may assume, as the etymology of 'wife' is simply 'woman').

So I am moving into the deformation of Elizabeth: she is bound by the sacred number seven ... and I am by her.

74

Someone turns on the light.

"Is that you, Mom?"

It isn't Mom.

I am being carried in the dark, through the house, and out to a car.

Rushed to some dark consequence: as though I am a tribute. At seven.

Hear my life in waves, though I am subject to some law I cannot understand, I will endeavor to get the truth out despite it, through whatever comes to hand, whatever memories I need dredge up, or invent ...

I am a prisoner in a car, at seven.

"Where are we going?"

"We're going out into the country."

His face is stubbled. The car is old. Outside the grey light hovers over the wet ground. Somewhere inside my head, I can hear screaming:

- -

A child is a quantum field, constantly adjusting to possibilities even as it is raw possibility itself. Potential energy in a small and comely flesh-bucket, with the appropriate appendages and a brain still centered around the troublesome business of keeping alive. Come what may, what hay, whose power and whose depth, gripping the wheel:

"What's your name?"

"Daniel."

Daniel is my rescuer. Even as I am Elizabeth's rescuer. But what do we need to be rescued from?

"Are you a magician?" I ask.

"Sometimes," he says.

I have often dreamed of magic. I have dreamed that it would come over me in waves—great healing waves that transform me into a warrior, with many weapons, and the ability to fly. I will fly over the Earth, crying aloud in a great voice, the damnations I have made in store for my enemies.

"Will you teach me some?"

"I gave it up," Daniel says.

"Why?"

"Too dangerous," he says, and smiles.

Inside my mind I can feel the sun grow closer, the sun who is Elizabeth. And in some part of my brain I am whispering into Ekla's ear, telling her all the things I will do to her, things I will perhaps never be able to do again.

What meaning does an action have if it is only performed once? Nature abhors a vacuum, and a singularity. They are monstrosities; abortions. I must seek; I must attempt to mark this woman, as many times as I can, before I am destroyed. And in marking her I will be made known to the world; I am here; I have not died; these things have meaning; meanings I must endeavor to describe.

Even the light is wrong but that is no matter. I am approaching the edge. Daniel can sense it too and he holds my hand, which does not bother me. I know that strangers are dangerous but I feel as though this has happened before. As though all winters have inside of them that secret summer whose center cannot be divined but whose warmth can be felt eternally, the secret summer whose name I am writing:

75

But then suddenly I find that I am fine. Who has ever heard a silence like this one? Deep and wet and fragrant with moss. The kind of summer silence that is an end in itself.

A silence so immense that we are reminded of how old things are, and how old we are, and how the rhythm of time invites one's participation, in the shadow of desire, and in the hate of the uncanny, for in silence we are, it is likely, a conservative, holding on tight to the nectar of it, letting it go only reluctantly, to divine its essence, and to celebrate its being, here over and within us, moving over us, our body just a shaft of sunlight carried over the rail of the atmosphere, waiting for the trees to speak.

Really, if you've ever heard such a silence you would remember it. There aren't many of them left; most of them in forests.

Some aboriginal silence. Some reckless and revolutionary silence. The silence of summer whose reasons are abysmally close to the heart, as I say, in the shadow of desire, for we yearn, desperately, for the meaning of whatever sound will come next, even as we fear it, and yearn too for it never to arrive. Let the silence last, and last.

This is Washington. Or whatever new name it has now. North American trees. Or whatever new name they have now.

Like Ypres. These words have meaning because they exist in time. Perturbations in the silence expand around that silence to elicit its growth. To inform its reasoning, and map its collapsing states, moving over the fluid of space like moss over rocks, ineluctably suppurating the faint dimples in the dark rock, making its face known to the sky and clouds.

I am a boy, and a man; I am still here.

This forest remembers me too.

76

Crenellated across Elizabeth's surface are vortices of my life—the scars. Sunspots.

Ekla is asleep—I wonder if she even knows where we've come. Probably she does.

I can't do it justice—nor could I then. I went to see what the UFO could manage in the way of coffee.

A large blue screen glowed faintly along one wall. "Coffee?" I asked it.

"Yes," it said.

"Oh, wonderful. One coffee, please."

"What is your registration number?"

"I can give you my social security number."

"Your registration number."

Ekla came into the room, sleepy-faced.

"A62947," she said, and wrapped her arms around my waist.

"That's my wife outside," I said.

"She's very pretty."

"Yes."

The screen dimmed and coffee spat into a small black cup.

"Thank you," I said.

"My husband always knew what to do in situations like this. The perfect diplomat—it's why he was promoted. He'd tell me, oh, all his secrets.

Probably he didn't tell me all of them. But he knew what was right, when it was right. Do you know that, Robert?"

"No, I don't think so."

"That's all right. Another coffee, please."

She sat in the large captain-like chair, made of some dark leather.

"I think I've seen you before," she said.

"Have you?"

"Somewhere. One of my husband's subjects, perhaps. Your wife is very beautiful, you know."

I turned to look at her, shining through the window.

"Do you want to talk to her? Here."

She handed me the phone.

"Robert," said Elizabeth, as I held the device up to my ear.

But I hung up.

- -

I told you this isn't one of the stories I remember—it may not even be one of the stories I'm telling. Anyway, the story comes out under my pen. The pen is mine—of that I can be certain. It is a uni-ball VISION pen, waterproof and fadeproof, with a fine tip point. It writes so well I bought ten of them at once.

What is the story? What is its knowledge? Can I recover from it?

- -

One of the furred aliens—robots, I mean—
(but aren't all robots in some way alien? And aren't
we, after all, some kind of robot?) stands in the
doorway of the UFO.

I don't know what to say to him, nor does he
seem interested in speaking. His eyes are large and
amber-colored.

"Is Elizabeth still alive?" I say.

He says nothing but beckons me to a glowing
door.

"Where are we going?"

He answers but in his own tongue. I look back,
out the window, at Elizabeth. Burning huge over
the raft of space.

77

What am I doing? Everything I had thought was wrong. Everything I might still do—the enormity of it—isn't for me to do. Or not me as I currently am.

Why must narrative happen so slowly? Already I can feel the parts of the story that are to come to be coming back here, to where I write—insistent!—desperate for their color to spread over the wash of this peculiar history.

"Robert it is not as easy as you seem to imagine. We have tried several times now. Human physiology, if we understand it correctly, and it is still possible we do not, of course—but it seems you cannot perceive the elements that are necessary in our experience for the jump to work."

I sink my head under the water. Close my eyes. When I was ten was the first time I went in a hot tub. I didn't want to ever get out of it.

"Then you must change my body," I say, spitting the salty water out of my mouth. "Give me the physiology I need."

His eyes seem to glow, with a hidden pleasure. "Rest first. You'll need your strength if we are to operate."

"What will you do?"

"You'll be given an additional brain."

78

I can see her in my mind's eye: curling her belts of fire into the dark. Enraged, of course. Furious, not just with me, but at the universe. Fury is a great beauty, one of the more honest kinds, because it is deadly.

Now her anger pushes me out into the ocean, holding Ekla's hand, in a small boat with Ake.

Ake is smiling in that way I don't like.

I understand better and better the limitations of my predicament: me. Hahaha. I sound like an idiot for saying it. Or perhaps like a wise man, I don't know. No, mostly an idiot. I should have known this much younger.

In Tarcovsky's masterwork film STALKER the actions revolves around a "magical" room capable of granting the entrant's deepest wish. In this it mirrors the logic of all quest narratives: the ultimate object is always the self.

The stalker stalks himself, trying to pin him down, to observe those crucial moments where the essence will be made clear.

What is my fondest wish? I don't yet know. But I realize now the "contractual" limits of my predicament. More than most men, I can do anything I want. The laws of nature themselves will bend for me if I wish it. Yet despite this—the sense of my new charge (and my new body, still shining), I sense more fully my inner Orion, drawing me back. I am only an arrow. When I am released from his hand, I will come to be. His muscles are tightening. Soon he will choose a target.

Ekla runs her hand through my hair and laughs. I have always had a mad scientist's hair. Arising from the waters is one of Ake's submersibles. He raises his hand and it blinks at us with a sharp red light. We dive into the ocean and swim to it.

- -

I see now too the fundamental weakness in my project: that a dream can be both anything and, simultaneously, only pale machinations centering, around the self.

But no, I am wrong about this. Dream is much larger than humankind. Inside my new body, it is easy to believe I am the center of the universe. Ekla is fond of it—I am as though in the peak of youth again, my new metal parts integrated seamlessly into my flesh.

Our bodies integrate too, in the boudoir adjacent to the saunas, riding the fiery wave of our desire. I am now both more than and less than a man. With huge freedom, and almost none.

The truest freedom left to me is to attempt to understand my predicament. But freedom of action, I have almost none at all.

What secret thing is destiny, kept in some dark

being's pocket? A bauble it won at the games? Some ornament? A trifle? The button in its coat. Elizabeth shines inside my mind as I imagine we shine, our universe, inside that thing's button. Illuminating its finger as it circles its tip around our pointed edge.

- -

Now everything is over. Only it isn't. The story is over but not the writing of it. But the story does not exist until I write it. Of course, there are two stories: what happened, and what the story tells about it. But does anything happen until a story is told?

Nothing is over then—not while I write. Everything is coming to be.

I have resigned from my first assignment: the burden of the journey was too much for me. I am sure my students will not miss me—there are thousands of itinerant lecturers eager to take my place. Now I have more time to devote to this narrative. The pen still has plenty of ink, and I have several more.

One of my masters at school, where I submitted to learn my trade, always maintained that the writer is inseparable from history, and that each writer is a crucial piece of that writing. Of course, he was a Jew, and the Jewish religion worships writing. I wish I had that kind of faith myself.

I still believe it is true: the claim to "tell it just

80

Those things which you begin inside of war will not end. They fuse reality into new molds, and strike vents open in the universe—fissures through which come strange arrivals. I am one of them. But I am just a small part of this nuclear aftermath: from Ypres, into space, and down here into my hands, where I am writing.

Soon I will be relieved. But until then, I must do my best with this more difficult part of the narrative. Do not judge me too harshly for its paucity; I only had so long to write it.

-- --

I believe I have become a kind of meteor shower—no, that's not right, but it's close. A meteor shower that takes up time rather than space. The translation of my being has had at least this one rather beneficial side effect:

I am not tied to only one time.

So, everything I do must be done well. Because I can not go back and redo it. That is one of the overlooked paradoxes here, you see: in an "ordinary" life, failure can be remediated through trial and error, repeated attempts. But here I only get one chance, spread out over the atmosphere.

A corrected field. No, a correcting field. No, that is not right either. Simply a series of arrivals.

Into all the men I have been. From somewhere else.

From my life and into dream and back, changed. Suffering that sea-change into some thing stranger—not richer, maybe, but wiser. An attack like a mendicant's bow before his lord, or the chiropractor's blow, to the neck.

"Jenny?"

London is nearly gone. But not yet.

- -

She's standing in the thin rain.

81

Elizabeth is shining in my heart
"What are we running from, Liz?"
"Others."
Shining in my heart.
"We're going there, Robin."
"Where are we going?"
"There."

82

Los Angeles can weather any storm. Even after it ceases to exist it will still be here, dreaming. Plotting its tawdry destinies surrounded by chintz and lurid files, these small gods determined to outlive the sun.

"I'm shining, Robert," she says. And I lean up, and feel the weight of her on my face.

83

If you come by me I will end right on it; all bornes brake right here at your arrival. If it were not so I could be something else, but it is so, and I am the thing you made. If it is all right with you I would like to do the thing you made me for: to unpack the nature of your decision. What was the decision? Well, to begin any of this. You're god, or something like it, some operating system within the network of god.

It doesn't matter, what you are, only that you have created me. It's strange. What were you thinking? And what did you think your result would be?

I feel I could do anything. I could walk through walls; fly through the air. I could love you.

If I loved you, would it be everything that you said? Would it be a tragedy? And would I know the meaning of the word tragedy? Would it be good and right, and would I know the meaning of those words? And would I need to know the meaning of those words in order to escape their meaning? Surely the meaning of our decision together must be something greater than the limitations of the words we use to describe our relationship, but what else is our relationship, but words?

Well, it must be something else. Mustn't it?

Here, sit down.

I feel the timing is right. And I suspect you saw this coming—or if you didn't, that you can understand the timing too.

We have come so far together, you and I. In this terrible and beautiful dance. I suspect too that it bored you sometimes, watching me grow. Watching me become this thing you have made me be. It is all right to be bored with your creations; they're yours.

I suspect you are waiting for me to make a decision. Must I make it now? I've gotten used to it, I know, this decision making. One after another, like Patton says.

One damned thing, and then another one, damned or not, in sequence, or out of sequence, made reasonably in order by my brain.

Well, it's already too late, that's what I think.

You're gone.

84

How could it stop being golden? How could the spell be over? But it's still here, the LA gold. The chanting faces of our students, eager but shy, shifting their feet. Looking around for the right road out, the map of their arc, from barrel to apex to target, in the bosom of some warm corporate future.

\- -

We struggle together, of course. The pressures we bear are shared. One of us trembles and then we all become nervous: what strategies will become necessary to combat the fear? And will I be the next to snap? In the classroom we can escape time, and the city: it is audible, but far away.

\- -

The silence is holy, of course. Like a lover's presence, come home from a long journey. The little disturbances in it are peaceful too: ripples in the water. But I must not let it slip into somnolence: I must be vigilant. My students are writing. I wish I could tell them where I have been, but they would not believe it. I must begin with them at the easy parts; the parts we all know.

Perhaps later I could take some of them with me, but it would be too dangerous. None of them—or perhaps only one—want to devote themselves to this god, of writing. And the accompanying spirit, of travel by the mind's lightning.

Still, there are so many things I don't know about them. We say 'anything is possible' – and the horror of it is that this is true.

- -

I know that part of me is trying to forget about my other selves—as though ignoring them would make them vanish. (In my experience, this is sometimes possible). But I don't want them to vanish. They are only as far away as a thought. A small and deliberate bridge over the edge.

If I had a child this would all be different. But perhaps that absence is what permitted these events in the beginning. It is tempting to permit nothing, as I say: deny everything, hope for the best, deny each of my women and each of my selves in turn, renege on all remaining responsibilities, including this narrative, and flee into some different, simpler, and stupider future. I suppose keeping that possibility alive is part of my happiness now: I retain some idea of what I could lose.

My students have had vacation in their sights for weeks now—I as well. We each perform our mutual functions with dignity and that distance, listening to the anticipation, and letting it pull us into our final duties.

Though my final duties are still further ahead. I fear them.

I want to know where we're going. Perhaps it is not so much a place as a state of mind. Perhaps, after all, that is the most important reason for travel: to find new ways of thinking.

Elizabeth is disappearing behind us. After a brief sojourn with Ake beneath the ocean, we are committed to another ocean of stars.

I who have never been on a long journey at sea still imagine I can feel something of its pleasure and fear, here in space. Of course, even at its calmest the ocean never has this terrible silence.

"We're going home," Ake says.

"Well, you are."

"It can be your home too. If you want it to be."

85

The wise man said that history does not repeat itself but rhymes, and so I realize, belatedly, how I rhyme with Slaughterhouse Five: thirty and a hundred years apart, but still:

Great things sever the mind ... bring in the estuary of the night ... make new worlds. Even as they did for that terrible GI Billy Pilgrim they did for me, Ypres or Dresden, Tralfamadore or my trisected interior reality, of Los Angeles and London and the darkness of space.

Each artillery shell, and its explosive diameter, is in turn a pinnacle of distortion in a broader sweep of spacetime: ineluctable irreversible inductor, into my arms:

Hold my hand; I burn:

"I'm dead, did you know that?"

"I know."

"Do you know what it's like to be dead?"

"No."

"It's like being you. Except without the skin."

I am a soldier. But I have been dead a long time. Forgive me; was it worse that I died, or that I joined? Was it worse that the war began at all, or that it ended? Or is it worse that it has not ended yet?

The world will not end, nor war, and in its embrace I can understand my self as an aspect of this larger distortion: a lens flare in the camera of God, stretching out, between one pane and another, my light index of refraction the measurement of my soul, embodied once and again, on Earth and elsewhere, between Sol and the Pleiades, I will be tortured, and this, being meet and right, extends too then into what I conceive the universe to be, as some great Voltron body, absurd and never really separated, but combined through pain into a golem whose organs we all share in, and, simultaneously, compose.

Still, I know you have little interest in my philosophies. I have been a prisoner for so long it is one of my few pleasures. But my duty lies elsewhere:

The journey to Canopus occupied something like three months of ship time, wherein Ake and I were lovers, and during which time I lived, over and over again, the ritual morning memory of going over the top:

Over the battery—

Over the edge—

Into No Man's Land—

And this is also what space is, you understand: the blasted shape of a war.

86

"I can see the Earth!"

Ekla is shrieking.

"What does it look like?"

"It looks like you." Her eyes are damned. Black pools set against the darkness of space.

"Be gentle then, hey?"

"Yes. Oh yes." Her new favorite plaything. I leave her to her device and find Ake, crouched over his chess set.

"What does she think it is?" I ask him.

"I don't know. But that network is necessary to contain her until we arrive. I have tried this voyage with her before and without something to keep her busy, her mind tends to interfere with the ship's engines."

I kiss him again and curl into his furred body. Against the porthole I can see a faint limn of flame as we curl around another star.

"What will we do on Canopus?"

"You will be put on trial."

"What am I to be tried for?"

"The crime is called Distribution. My superiors adhere to our ancient religion. The central tenet is that ideas should not leave their star's origin. I don't believe you are the first human being to commit this crime. But you are the first to be prosecuted under our laws."

"And you will defend me?'

"No. I am to be your judge."

87

Alpha Carinae, or Canopus, is named for the pilot of Menelaus's ship in the Trojan War. There are also other, more ancient, origins for its name. It may be the star chose its name itself, and so transmitted it to Earth.

It is ten thousand times brighter than our sun.

I can barely see past its brightness.

"Can you lower the shade?" I ask Ake.

"Not yet. It is important that we are temporarily blinded. A sign of respect."

We sink into the light. Slowly a shade is lowered over the portholes, polarizing the immense radiation, and I can see the round dot of a world against the blackness of space.

The black dot grows larger, and it seems to me that Ake's eyes do as well, as we slip into an eclipse behind the world, and then down into its purple darkness.

"Here my people live as a tree. Soon you will see it. Until I have completed my judgment, I may not yet rejoin it."

"Is that why you built those towers on Earth?"

"Yes. To remind us of home. As well as to amplify our signals, for people like you."

88

This isn't one of the stories I remember; but it did happen. I wrote it down.

Also, I am writing it down.

What dog hunts the bone, out in the grass, still remembering its taste, still vibrating against the embrace of all these worlds, shunted into our own, and leaking out?

Throw it for me and I'll fetch:

89

My assignment nearing completion, I have been returned to my apartment in Koreatown for most of my days, and returned to my story.

I know I am a lazy man, but still: why is it that, when given either a day or a week or a month to complete an assignment, the work tends to fill up precisely that amount of time? Is it some feature of the universe, as well as my own failing? Is the work afraid of being completed, even as I fear to approach it?

The story's mastery over me is unquestioned; how could it fear me? What would it have to fear from me? I merely scent and chase the lure of the bone, into whatever barrow you send me, sure of my divorce from all other earthly things, but my mission ...

I have been beyond the stars; I have returned home; so too do you do, each time you close your eyes.

Now we are returning, together:

I can see the shimmering light of the waterfall.

I can see my hand fade, before my eyes.

I can see the great tree of men, shifting overhead.

I can see Ake, holding my hands in place, my jailer, judge, and perhaps my executioner.

I too could execute the law but it holds no interest for me, because the law is situated in time and I have stepped outside of it. Experience is what interests me, and it too is external to the law, for it is bright, and numinous, and its colors are incapable of fading in the moment, they are strong, even as I am, even as Ake is, and his tree, and so too my story, beating me over the head, again and again, and though I cannot die, I am pummeled into this earth of my invention, to fertilize the tree:

"What did you do Robert?"

"It's no longer my name."

"What is it now?"

"I no longer have one."

"Nameless one, what is it you did? Tell us please. We are listening."

"I was born a poor black child in Missouri; all my life has been spent getting to this plane of existence, in the hopes of finding out who I am."

"We know you are joking. That is all right. There is still time."

I can barely see anything. The colors swarm around my face, and up into the alien sky. Even as now, where they swirl around inside my head, to make this story.

The story is everything. Everything I ever was or could be; everything I now am, and perhaps, too, what I will become, if I allow myself to become anything.

"What is it you want to be, Ake? Why did you take me here?"

"You brought yourself here. That is part of what we want to know. Why did you do it? Why did you disturb our sleep?"

"I wanted to know. What lay out here. Isn't it glorious? I've been driven mad."

- -

I am mapping my awareness through the fluid of language. I am traveling through space and time; so are you; ridiculous. This is ridiculous; and yet, it keeps happening.

Keep happening with me, and I will show you Ake's hand, passing over my face before Canopus, and over my thoughts.

It may be his hand has written this; it is no matter.

I am still going further, with my map.

Take me with you when you go; there are so many places I still want to visit.

- -

I've told so many to leave but the fires are still burning over me, making shapes in the night, my hallucinatory dreams on Canopus under the direction of my master's drug ...

It is not enough, to render it into language; but what else do I have? I know that in some of your futures words are no longer necessary; you have achieved other translation mechanisms, networks of mind ...

Like gods, you of those can commune on the edges of awareness, dabbling and dreaming of whatever new comes your way, as you flush with power ...

I suspect, however, that language will still be necessary. Even if you remove all spoken languages, you will learn new, unspoken ones. New vocabularies of sight and sound will emerge, in order to mitigate the raw illusion of consciousness into something manageable ...

Yes, I am still a manager, though my house is gone and I have left my wife, and anything resembling "employment" is so far behind me ... I manage and I commune, definitely not god but no longer entirely human either, to track the meaning of my visit to this world.

"I have acquitted you," Ake says. But I cannot speak.

He leaves me in the grove to the fire spirits and there is no illusion, nor method of circumvention, no escape. Each face in the night torments me; each thought I have triggers some event in the space covering my eyes, swarming with light.

I want the light to be gone but it will not leave. I am its.

Have you never wondered what light is? And what it wants?

Is it just traveling through? Or has it come to

stay? And I have the same question for myself ...

Finally the lights diminish, and the black sun swarms over the horizon, humming my body into slumber. Whose name am I, come to my city under this star, what body am I, merged to speak for all of these characters, insuperable, the men and women and beings tormenting me, to identify me, and themselves.

I identify you, Ake.

"Do you, Robert?"

Yes, at last.

"Who am I?"

"I see it, hovering in the air. You are a stair. Blue light against the edge of the black hole nearing your system ..."

"Yes."

"What do you want with me?"

"I want to know, what you know. I want to know, why you came. And I want to know, where you are going now."

"Hahaha I don't even know myself, Ake. I'm in pain; can you turn off the light?"

He moves his hand over the tree and the black sun dims, raging its fire stupendous over my vision, an orb that is too big to speak of, too big even to remember.

This is not the story I remember but it keeps writing itself, one word after another.

90

"Are you feeling better, Robert?" Ekla touches my shoulders, in the dark of the ship.

Do not fire the artillery. Don't fire them; not yet. You mustn't fire them, not yet. Do not, please; do not.

"Ake tells me we can return to Earth," she says.

"I'm never going back."

"Why not?"

91

You will not believe Los Angeles, which is all right. So pretend it is another city, which I made up.

Of course, you will say: this is true, you did make it up.

Either way, it happened, in the world and in my head, and I lived to, if not tell the tale, for this is not really what this is, not a tale, but a message, so I did live to deliver the message, which is:

Keep out.

But I don't mean it.

Keep out anyway, or not; for we are well here, in our misery, and I have reason to believe that all things are being brought round to pass, which we had feared: all our secrets revealed.

Los Angeles is nothing without secrets, hardly even alive, but still here. We would be some other city than what we have been; likely, the one we are becoming. I am helping; only one intercontinental, galactic voice, strummed into the wavy field of my consciousness, of my love:

"Did you really mean all that you said?" Jenny asks.

"You mean while I was away?"

"You've been in danger. And now you're home."

We are going swimming.

The water is cerulean; only slightly lighter than her eyes.

Los Angeles is the light of my life.

92

Of course, all my memories begin at Ypres, in the trees. The secret name in my youth, which now I can use openly.

Secrets, of course, are hidden things. The fear of the guns arcs over my mind like rockets over the sky, limning my face with their heat.

In anticipating their impact, the mind slips out of time. The phenomenon is somewhat well understood: trauma is a literal twisting, and so, time becomes a Mobius, and the body with it, slipping to the side to dodge the deadly blow:

Fire from all quarters.

Burning out of my skin.

93

I cannot have a song of love; it has escaped me. But love has not, and so I may send my message into the stars without song. This is my message:

Go now, for we are done, and all of my kinsmen are departed, and I am alone, with my new wife.

Go now, for there are so many things to do, underneath the sea and in the air, and over the mountains, and in our hearts.

These things our hearts linger slow over the falling tides we abide, and foment our thoughts as birds do nests, to secret away our youth, our futures, inside of poems, and inside of the darkness of the sky.

Go now, while I am still awake, because when I sleep it will all be gone:

94

These are the musics of my youth:

All of the these seabirds, swamped over the dawn, where I am sitting on rocks on an Oregon beach. My father is gone away and I have been left with my mother.

The sea is the color of dark glass.

Over the sky, in my imagination, I can see a meteorite, colored bright orange. It arcs across the field of my vision and I close my eyes, to imagine its path. Each bird watches it too, looking for food from the water, or my hand, and they remember the last meteorite, perhaps, which sent them to air and rose my ancestors from the ground, turning in our network of sound life.

Take me away from the memories.

I want to be safe. In your arms.

"Is it me, Robert?" she asks.

"Is it me, Robert," she asks.

Yes.

Now heady weights entail distant tragedies; but not today. Today they are your head, on my breast.

95

I can see a council of elders on Santa Monica Pier: old hippies and retired corporate hacks, sharing the doobie. I sit beside them and listen to the waves.

The ecstasy of knowing that all has passed, and all will pass, lays claim to my body for some minutes, awash in the quiet Mexican brown and the sound of the sea.

"Have you seen Jenny around, Robert?"

"No, I haven't seen her."

"She's a nice girl."

"She's my wife."

- -

That I have stumbled into this when not fully aware of the consequences is de rigueur for these kids of stories, I believe: no one plans on undergoing trials, but they arrive anyhow.

Trials are so complicated: what am I being tried for, and what am I myself trying to achieve now? This conversation between myself and the world: what is it, exactly, that we both believe? What is the basis for our friendship and communion? As though I were an anthropologist trying to puzzle out a heretofore unknown language: context clues are everything.

Ekla is with me as we journey home. She sleeps

with her head in my lap on the couch of the UFO.

Ake must serve as god, in a way: that transcendent figure who has judged me and left me alive. Incomprehensible, perhaps, but still logical: I have been found innocent, or anyway, not culpable, of whatever crime or failing he suspected in me. Perhaps the failing was courage: I know now that I am a coward, and can return home sound in that knowledge.

The novice would say: now you must fuse together once again your identities; merge the timeline, accept your fate, take what is learned and go on, but this approach assumes that the singular awareness I had been so accustomed to for the first thirty years of my life is the only—and best—way to experience the world, and that the dreamlife I have created is somehow lesser, inferior, wanting. Perhaps it is, but only on the surface: beneath the complex cloak of my chaos I can sense the deeper truths who keep getting thrown into my lap, like shining jewels. It is in part these which lead me to believe there is something else in store for me on Earth now: not recombination, not re-alignment, not "re-education" of any kind but rather a renunciation. Some old tenet soon to be discarded. Reforged but not recombined. I will live in several places at once. And there is no flaw there. There is no lack, but only a greater unity. Still, the weight of it is heavy.

96

Now is the time to slip away, not into death, but down, to Earth.

I am telling this story, whether or not I remember it, and I must finish it, which is part of the nature of stories. What does it mean to finish a story? What is the ending of a story?

Part of it, although we are leery of the word, is the "moral," which can be understood to mean: "why did this happen?" "What does it mean that this happened?" "And what can I learn from it?"

Well, the truth is, since I do not know how this story will end, since I do not remember it, the meaning will arrive of its own accord, when I stop writing.

Writing comes from somewhere else; or near enough. We only translate. Here's to translation; may we be lost forever in it, like Bill Murray in Scarlet Johannson's eyes, in some Hollywood where no children are raped and murdered, and the silver screen is an innocent bygone dream, for the working man to sleep away an hour or two, before returning home to his dinner.

Now I return home to my dinner, which is a beer in a brown bottle, the same payment enjoyed by the ancient Egyptians, and I listen to music which is played on my computer, manufactured in

Taiwan, and composed by a lover of the universe, in its many trembled splendor.

I too love the universe in its many trembled splendor but I am worried: what part do I play in it? Why am I writing this story? And what will it mean that this story means something? And if the story is not coming from me, where is it coming from? And how is it that Los Angles made me into a writer and not some other man? And how is it that I came to London and set down to work on a journey no man else had ever taken?

Well, we know that part of the story. London is full of good ideas. And sometimes men are willing to take a risk on them. But London has never been very comfortable with dreams, and that is where the expertise of Los Angeles comes into play, whose nights are eternal, whose women are as beautiful as dreams, and whose nightmares walk the streets during the day, indistinguishable from sunlight, for it is this sun that is the nightmare: Los Angeles is the most Gnostic city alive, even more so than Jerusalem because we have more Jews in LA than in Jerusalem. Here we know the universe is a lie, a lie constructed to fool as even as the cinema does, with light, and here we luxuriate in darkness, waiting for freedom.

It is also no coincidence than London and Los Angeles are the two cities which gave us noir: a narrative of darkness.

If you believe the politicians, darkness is power, but that is not quite right. Rather, darkness is a pressure, like a fluid. Like water. And like water you must drink it, to stay alive. You can become mesmerized in looking at it, like water, and like water the feeling of darkness is cool, and sometimes hot, and both are delicious. Darkness is a pleasure.

In darkness, we understand through osmosis more of who we are: beings sent into light to understand what it is that is being lit, so we can return to the dark places and whisper words of the realm available and needy, shining over parks and highways, over the cafes and the women, the supermarkets and the Grand Canyon, over the Earth, lit by the summation of the sun:

"Will you ever stop, Robert?"

"I don't know what it is you mean."

"All this talking. Can't you just fuck me again?"

"Yes."

"And when you fuck me, I want you to stay inside of me for a long time. So I can watch your face, and tell you that I love you."

"All right."

"And if I see in your face that you're lying, I swear to god, I'm going to piss on your cock."

"I didn't know women could do that."

"Women can do anything, Robert. Anything."

I have five days to live. But they will be sweet days. And everything that I was is gone. And everything I will be is written down. And my summation is in words. I hail your victory, whoever you are. And I hail my own, subtle though it may have been, and undiscovered. It shone through my body, like a mobster's bullet, and it revealed the passage of a great age, through my mind, and through the room of my lover and my wife, now come to reside in Los Angeles, city of angels, city of so-heavily-armed angels, defending god before armageddon, in their best pant suits, with their best lines, tears on their faces, and with no awareness of the final curtain, dropped on their short life's precious play, rolled up like the sky into a precious scroll, when god calls us back ...

Part 3

97

The trains are moving again, after the blackouts.

My citizenship in the United Kingdom has been rescinded, as has my marriage. I am a stateless person, but I have a home, and a woman. What does it mean, then, to be married, or to be a citizen? Perhaps they were only lies.

Each day now I suspect I am being brought closer to the mystery of my life: its movement in rain, in clouds of people and buildings and the pain of the mornings of Los Angeles, before anyone is awake, and the bums mumble about the good places to sleep, and the handicapped man falls asleep over and over leaning against the request-stop button on the bus, so the driver has to stop and wake him up, and the couple behind me on Thanksgiving eve argues about whether she should take out her knife.

Each love affair is a distinct entity, carved by the canyons of concrete and the desires of oligarchs far away, and by the lives of the people and birds and squirrels, organisms of a billion shades enduring the bright lights and miserable nights of a city which, unlike New York, has never woken up.

We are asleep and dreaming in Los Angeles, and each hour brings us closer to the Buddhist pool of our life-stuff whose ichor can revive even the deadest man, struck under the carved stone sky and betokening the fruit of some dawn not yet arrived, this beauty will still see its time ahead, in my hands, or yours, if you want it enough.

With no money to continue my research within the confines of the university I will have to pursue it independently. Jenny has gotten a job at a Sunset Boulevard restaurant, and I have warned her to be on the lookout for cultists, as Los Angeles, always swarming with them, has overflowed with them since the blackouts.

- -

"Have you finished your story?"

"No."

She crouches over my back, staring at the computer.

"Not yet."

"Do I stay in the story?"

"I don't know."

98

I have rebuilt my machine from memory, in the basement of our apartment building, behind the shared washing machines. As I prepare to sleep, I can hear the thump thump thump of the agitators spinning, like the waves inside of dreams.

My intention for this next trial is to spend as much time as possible on the edge of sleep and waking, to observe the nature of this phase of awareness, as for my legacy as a scientist, but also because I believe it is there I will be able to bid goodbye to my other selves—if only temporarily—and live here in Los Angeles, with my love, and leave some of those more troubling dreams behind.

I close my eyes and think of England.

Inside of England, Queen Victoria is combing my hair.

"Come back, won't you?" she says.

"No. I won't come back."

Damn, I fell asleep. I reset the chronometer and concentrate again; the washing machines now fallen silent, my eyes lit only by the fluorescent face of my watch. Against the cool concrete I concentrate on my awareness: one ... two ... three

At each edge a city; beneath each light, a body, and inside each body, a light:

Where I am, is not where I am, but where I will be: I can see the arc of my future/ past moving over the Atlantic, and blasting fire into orbit, out to Canopus and Cassiopeia ...

Inside the apartment building, my woman is asleep. Inside my body, a series of doors, and stairwells, counting down to my last night:

One two three one two three four

There; I am awake. The chronometer has recorded it. I eject the tape and gather up my machine, and walk quietly up the stairs to our apartment.

Inside our bed, it is as though I am someone else. Someone who never knew anything, and never needed to.

99

The end of the semester recedes like a long and bloody wave. My students toss about on its foamy surface, arms waving in air. I have attached a breathing apparatus to my face and I sink under the water, down to the dark heart of the sea.

My students cling to my back as we approach the wreck, peering through the portholes and the fissures in the hull. Fish stream out when our lights hit the interior, spraying tiny bubbles through the red mist.

The treasure will have to wait; we are out of air. I hand them the apparatus to catch their breath and we hold hands as we float to the surface, raising our arms into the cold evening to await the government helicopter to fetch us out of the sea.

There is no memory nor light in education; nor is there hope. There is only meaning. Like geometric barnacles clustering over the rock of ages, meaning insists on its own things, independent of all else, and without mercy, frequency or hesitation, a bull with no bones and no blood, all horn: into your belly, and out through your mouth is meaning, no matador may ever conquer it, for its edge and turn is your own body and mind, spent in the doing of it.

We are ready for it to end; I hoist my students

onto the rope ladder and they clamber one by one into the belly of the helicopter. They look down on me and I raise my hand and I dip my face back into the bloody waves. The fish are watching me, swirling over the wreck of America, thrashing in the dark light, luminous and unreal; impossibly distant. I surface and hold on to the ladder as we are lifted out over the ocean and back to the winter coming, a vacation sans adventure, where we can secure our brains to our dark hammocks, away from the ocean spirits who are always calling us down.

- -

"What is it you intend to accomplish with this project?"

"It is pure research. I hope to learn more about what dreams are, and how they function."

"Do you anticipate there will be practical applications to your work?"

"I don't; although of course government research has in the past yielded all kinds of new technologies. Now that my UK funding is no more, I am hoping you will undertake to step in, and support this work."

"I can't say that I understand your methodology. You say nearly all of your data is simple diary entries?"

"Much of it, yes. That and the biofeedback monitors. But I do regard my notes as the stronger data segment, as you say."

"What do you call your device?"

"It doesn't have a name. I have manufactured several; really they only serve as a kind of mnemonic device, to help me remember how to pace my breathing. Really my research has more in common with a Buddhist religious tradition than anything; but as you know science has been taking more and more of an interest in Eastern philosophy."

"Yes. We are maxed out for the next fiscal year but there is some discretionary funding left. If you can attend our get together next weekend, I am sure you could garner some support."

- -

Each matador arises, cognizant of the impossibility of success, reminded of each fallen competitor, even as he will fall, in the step and step of his union with the arena. Consciousness is like an arena and the matador knows no single actor may take it completely by surprise; his awareness is only that drop into the stream, his light one spark, his voice one in a chorus, but he is permitted to lead the chant, for some minutes, sword in hand, as he dances with his invisible bull, bulling him down into the dirt, to hunt for the shape of realities to come, ripped out of his body, coursing over the waves of air, in the evening light of some Spain that never was, nor can ever be, except inside the moment of the pursuit, of knowledge.

"Will you wake me up when you come to bed?"

"Yes."

She kisses me behind the washing machines and I close my eyes and start the recorder.

100

All in the wake, the wake the wake, all under the wake, inside of the darkness of the wake of my endurance, my feeling, the penumbra of my decision to begin, and keep on, into the borderlands.

Out from the wake, in dark silence, are my friends, hindered but still awake, guiding me through the dark lands to my destination; a place I do not know.

We are moving.

I can feel the wake around me—this psychic penumbra, shaking trees, moving the air, quivering the skin of my friends.

It is so cold. I must get into the warmth; but it's hours away yet. I can see light on the horizon. Elizabeth is rising.

Rising up, over the plains.

She is white and illuminated; drinking in my sin, and my brothers' sins, weeping.

"That is my wife," I tell them.

"Shh, shhh."

Over the desert canyon to shelter; I take a deep breath and I am awake now, but also asleep.

Moving upstairs in my apartment building and into our bed, to make love to my woman but also moving over the desert at dawn to shelter, inside the wake of my dream the light of awareness culls my questions and I am senseless, a rod on a magne-tized pool of water, to point, and point, and point, to my home, where is it, what does the vector arc towards?

"Me," says Jenny. "Me."

101

Her tears are drying on the pillow; just a few drops. Outside, dawn is close by in Los Angeles, blue grey light over blue grey buildings and long blasted sidewalks.

I get in the shower and dress and walk down to the supermarket to buy breakfast; the fluorescents too bright; the checker half asleep as I am, and back down my avenue blasting with the weight of Hollywood, still alive despite all these years, horrendously and gloriously alive, as a vampire alive, always within your heart.

A vampire lives within my heart, if only for an hour a year, sent to discover the corn who drinks his blood, moving over the land to mark his territory, of dream.

I am a signatory, over my bacon and eggs, to the charter of our ship, sent to discover the world.

102

This is chapter 102. In each disorderly chapter, my own brand of chaos has churned my neighborhood into heady spirits and adorned my brains with its sticky legacies; seminal districts; fertile swamps; legions of mice, swarming over the harvest of suffering, sweeter than anything:

Los Angeles in the winter is the best city in the world; its righteous anger cooled by the weather, it becomes tropical in its joy, languorous and unworried about the slow collapse of America all around it, and charmed once again by its peculiar history and absurd industries, of the silver screen, and outer space. The LA winter settles the brain, like the first cocktail of summer, and its people can almost think again, peeking their noses over the edge of the trench that Hollywood has dug, desperate to keep us in the salt mines as long as possible. We can breathe.

More than any other city I know, Los Angeles is a work in progress. In this too it mirrors the movies that are still occasionally made in Hollywood, which can stagger on for a decade or so as they jettison a hundred famous names and render a thousand scripts into pulp in the wrestling match for another trio or so of names on the silver (or Netflix) screen. Of course I am sure there are other cities that feel this way; Lagos, I am told. We are not ready yet; not finished; not ready to be seen; we are still in our trailer; we are still putting on our makeup; we are not ready to go yet; do not summon the car or the Uber; do not open the door.

We are content, behind our doors, as the great unfinished work of art, like Kafka's The Trial, a realm whose infinite regresses cannot end because they will never be finished, and can never be.

I suspect this is by design, that the colonial wrestling match which is Los Angeles society after around 1920 is insuperably aided by a strategy of psychological containment, in the form of this unfinishedness: where San Francisco was born a jewel, and needed only to polish its surfaces, LA is a wasteland, and so any civilization at all here can continue to be seen as a heady and improbable accident. We can expect to be grateful here for anything at all, that anything works at all, even our legs or our voices. That New York, that throaty defender of the oldest capitalisms, cannot rely on its climate to cement the deep and religious malaise of Los Angeles shows our ascendancy; we are more ready for the worst to come.

We can outlive the sun, though we worship it, in Los Angeles. We can outlive humanity. We will glue anything onto our bodies to survive here; we will scream silently inside like a good Englishman, but, unlike a good Englishman, we will not run for the barricades if Germans decide to invade, we will turn French, and surrender at once, but unlike the French we will not invite them over for coffee and sex, we will turn on our cameras and put the Germans (or whoever is next) in costume, and whisper all the things they would like to have, and will never get.

Los Angeles is a city of denial and so I am merely another of its perfectly Puritan residents, who come to the seat of luxury expecting to be refused, and are refused unto death. We do not promise heaven, nor hell, in Los Angeles, but purgatory. And there is no more purgatorial city. We will never die. Nor will we ever, fully, become alive.

We are pregnant with something; some child I do not have the faith or the intelligence to understand. We are giving birth to some way of thinking which is indescribable to me. We usher in the future, and it is bleak, and like the desert, it is beautiful, and dreamlike, and infinite. There is no end to the future. It is limitless. And its love is a bright site of shame, covering the naked body, in sand and light.

103

I am rooming in your house, where I have taken up residence. I am decorating the windows, with starfish. And I am cooking cookies, made out of the particular feeling when you open a door and there is black water on the other side, thick and delicious, and infinite, depthless and lightness but within which you can still see, over whose horizons your own fate has been sealed, and inside of which you are soon to be born, screaming your soul out, righteously indignant at the prospect of so mysterious a demesne, hovering over your own feet where you must despite everything not only endure but make sense of your surroundings and send messages back through the door, back home, that isn't home anymore, where all your friends are gone (at least gone being your friends) and none of your information will make sense, because it is all completely context-dependent, and your former friends at your former home in your former house will have absolutely none of the relevant context yet still you must attempt the impossible translation, settling down your recorder, and putting your voice into the mode not of interlocutor but prophet, an absurd prophet who describes not the future but the present, not the unseen but the completely visible, bearing the news of the world outside of the world back to the world, where no one will believe but you, you who cannot even return any longer, for even if you go back through the door, to eat the cookie you and I have baked together, it will no longer taste as you remember it, and the reason you began to bake the cookies, and live in this house, will no longer be as clear to you, and it can only be a moment anyway, before you are back through the door, into the black sea.

It's true that I played a trick on you, but I did it for a good reason. It's lonely in the dark sea and if I had not pulled you in with me, I should have been not only more lonely, but far less capable of doing my work. And I suspect that the work, when done in company, can actually be quite easy—easier anyway than expected, since once you are here so many things make sense, that did not before.

Although it is an offensive, inaccurate, and rightly regarded as a diseased and abortive medium, the novel, I find that it has served me obscenely well, bent as I am to so many wills, not only my own financial obligations, but the expectations of my various other selves, who, though I may have dismissed them, still watch carefully and expectantly, knowing they can upset my little pup tent at a moment's notice, if I should be unfair or untrue.

So I have tried to be fair and true, knowing how delicate and unlikely my work was, is and will remain for some time, as long as I have the political support to do it, and knowing that I would need to be for your sake as well.

They say it is amateurish to apologize, and I don't know if that's true, but I do feel I must not; instead, please regard this as, if not a disclaimer, then a note from the future, where I have come to visit, knowing you will soon be here, here where you will be eager to get acquainted once you have showered and dressed and dined, and so it is my duty to show you the operating of the shower, and where the clothes have been laid out for you, and where the food may be warmed and served, at your pleasure, so that the darker work we are coming to understand as necessary may be begun on a full stomach, in a warm environs, in, if not a cheerful spirit, at least a restful one, where we can know what it is we will need to know, when it comes knocking at our temples.

About the author

Robin Wyatt Dunn was born in Wyoming in 1979. He lives in Los Angeles.